BOOKS BY SKOOT LARSON

The Lars Lindstrom Zen Jazz Mystery series:

The No News is Bad News Blues

The Real Gone Horn Gone Blues

The Dig You Later Alligator Blues

The On the Road Again Blues

The Dave Holman "Texas" Mystery series:

Copkiller

The Texas Detective

The Pachyderm Predicament

The Ivory Coast Puzzle

Political Humor

Apollo Issue, a Humorous Look at Healthcare

The Palestine Solution

The Testament of Jessica Crystal

Fantasy

King Irv's Big Adventure

King Irv's Cabernet Caper

King Irv and the Holy Grail

A Humorous Fantasy

Skoot Larson

Skoot's
Jazz
Books

ISBN: 978-0-692-96363-0

Published by Skoot's Jazz Books

Rockport, Texas

For my three wonderful granddaughters; Amberly, Maegan and Lindsey, and my daughter, Kristin, wherever she may be...

And again, thanks to Theresa Feeser for her patience, editing and guidance.

Part I
The Convention

"So why did the chicken cross the road?" Morrie the Jester asked Hershel the Merlin.

"He saw a couple Christian missionaries coming outta the pub?" Hershel replied.

"Oh, okay, I must have told you that one before," Morrie frowned taking a drink of his ale. "So tell me again why you want to travel to Londres? It's a terrible place, full of filth and disease. I mean those people just toss the dross from their chamber pots out their windows into the streets to let the rain wash it away down the gutters to the river. And so many people everywhere you look? Oy! I wouldn't wish Londres on my worst enemy, are you kidding? They hated my jokes there, I mean I bombed big-time, me, Morrie the *Jester*. And you know how popular I am everywhere I've played around here. Are you ready for another pint yet?"

"No, I'm good," Hershel told him. "And I guess you'd say I have to go down there on business. They're having a Merlin convention. I mean where else would they hold it? Londres is supposed to be at the very center of our world."

"So why don't you convince them to have it here in Vaudeville? We're only about fifty miles north of Londres and our area could use the tourist business. Listen, we could hold it right here in the Vaudeville Playhouse just down the lane from this very pub and I could do *two* shows a *night* for an audience like that. And think of the ale and wine we could sell locally."

"Sorry, Morrie, my apologies to King Richard, but it wasn't my decision to make. I only learned about all this from Crazy Max, the Merlin over in Berten on Cherwell. Someone else planned all this some time ago. I'm just glad that I got an invitation. So what else can you tell me about Londres?"

"Yeah, okay. Let me get that barmaid's attention. Miss? Can I get another pint?"

"So you were saying about Londres?" Hershel pressed, waving his hands to draw the jester's attention back to their table.

"Well, watch out for pickpockets," Morrie told him, waving his empty tankard in the air and looking all around for their serving wench. "There're poor folks all over that city looking to steal your wallet or anything else they can grab from you."

"I'll be careful about that," Hershel told the aging comedian. "Actually, I don't plan to go walking around the town. I'll be staying pretty close to our little encampment with Max from over in Berten and our knights. I'm not looking for women of easy virtue or anything like that, I just want to talk with the other magicians from around the island."

"What?" Morrie exploded. "You're going to the big city and you aren't interested in the local crumpet? Hershel, what kinda man are you?"

"A focused man," the Merlin told him with a straight face. "Truth be told, I'd much rather all these people would come up here and save me having to travel anywhere at all."

The landlord's daughter appeared from the back smiling at Hershel the Merlin who shook his head that he didn't need another ale. She pulled a single pint and headed for their table as Morrie said, "Hershel, you are a strange one. I mean I've heard that from people, but I always just figured, well, you know…"

Morrie wagged his eyebrows at the landlord's daughter as she put a fresh drink down in front of him. He took a deep draught from the newly delivered tankard and put out a hand to slap the maiden's backside, but she sidestepped his pat with a loud, "Oh, you!" and a laugh.

"I can see where you might get into some trouble in the big town," Hershel chuckled, placing a handful of brass coins on the table to cover their drinks.

"Hey, I got some packing to do," he told the half-squiffy comic. "I'll see you later."

"Call me when you get back," Morrie shouted after Hershel as the Merlin headed for the door. "And if you hear any good new jokes in the city, write'm down for me. I'm always needing new material."

"You can say that again," Hershel mumbled under his breath as he walked out into the sunlit lane.

ONE

It was a lovely and clement evening in old blighty. A warm sun was setting just across the King's Highway and the Warehouse Castle golf course as King Irv putted his ball into the cup on the nearby and newly completed 18th green to finish his game just under par. He raised his head to grin at the members of his little foursome; Rabbi Weiss, his son-in-law, King John, and his young grandson, Prince David Irving. He'd been a bit disappointed that he couldn't locate his Merlin, Hershel, to join the game. He'd had to call Rabbi Weiss at the last minute to fill out the foursome, but now, as he hefted his bag of clubs onto his shoulder and headed back towards the castle, he saw Hershel busying himself outside his cave on the other side of the fairway.

"Hershel, old friend, where have you been?" the monarch called across the expanse of grass. "I haven't seen you in a day or two?"

The tall, red-headed king walked over to the Merlin's cave, winked a very blue eye and looked his friend up and down, taking in the man's highly polished boots and sparkling new white tunic, both very out of character for his kingdom's chief magician, usually a scruffy and unkempt presence.

"And what are you doing all dressed up like the dinner of a dog?"

"Well, Irv," Hershel replied, casting his eyes downward. "I got some interesting news by courier the other day from Max, King Bertie's Merlin. It seems that all the Merlins around our little island have decided to get together and have a convention. They've invited me to be a guest speaker. They want me to address the assembly on the subject of time travel."

"So, what's a convention? Is that like a large group of crows?" King Irv fired back.

"No, you're thinking of a *murder* of crows." Hershel told his king. "A convention is, like, a gathering of likeminded people, so this would be a gathering of *Merlins*, like royal magicians from all around our island. Do you remember how I showed you on that globe thingy of mine that your kingdom is sitting on the eastern edge of a big island? So, you know, all the best and brightest magical minds on this island of ours are coming together to share ideas."

"I didn't realize that you all knew each other," King Irv replied. "I mean, I hardly know any of the other kings beyond our little area. I *do* know that there are other realms north of the Hamptons, west of Berten on Cherwell and going south past Woburn Abbey toward Londres, but I've never had dealings with any of these lords."

"Well, that's because you're *kings*, Irv. You rule over people. Ruling over people is a simple art. You just have to look out for everyone's best interests and defend your patch of land. We men of magic, we deal in *science*. It's something that works best if we all share ideas, you know, tell each other about the experiments we've made so we can advance our knowledge without covering the same ground over and over again." Hershel hesitated. "Or maybe you wouldn't understand, not being a man of science yourself."

"Oh, I think I understand," King Irv told his Merlin. "I just never imagined that all these other kingdoms had people like you..."

"But you knew of Max, the Merlin in Berten on Cherwell, highness. I mean he's not a great example of a man of science, but then he's a Christian. I mean, I guess, it's hard to keep an open scientific mind when you believe all that Christian stuff."

"Now Hershel," his king scolded, "you've told me yourself that the key to learning is keeping an open mind…"

"Exactly my point," Hershel replied, making a face.

"I don't think Rabbi Weiss would approve…"

"It's okay, Irv," Hershel told him. "Me an' the Rabbi are tight. We just agree to disagree on certain things. Got time for a drink, highness?"

"I thought you'd never ask," chuckled the king. "I always enjoy sharing a bit of conversation with you over a pint."

ershel left early the next day, traveling south in a convoy with Max the Merlin from the neighboring kingdom of Berten on Cherwell. King Irv assigned a couple of his knights to join the traveling entourage although it was largely sponsored by the neighboring Christian kingdom. Hershel had been offered a place in their convoy because of the current interest in time travel and King Bertie's fears regarding his recent experience with time travelers who had come to his land searching for cabernet grapes that had been stolen from the future by two young brothers working for King Irv, determined to produce the Cabernet wine that his good lady, Queen Sophie, desired.

Irv and his grandson, DI, along with the royal tabby cat, Gaolbird, went to the edge of the King's Highway to see the entourage off along with King Bertie and Queen Agnes of Berten on Cherwell. Although the two monarchs were not really friends, they acted cordially towards each other and made small talk about what their Merlins might accomplish by attending this meeting. King Richard of Vaude, best friend of Irv's son Prince Sol and the Wholesale Kingdom's closest ally did not attend the gathering. Gaolbird the cat clung to the mane of Irv's silver stallion, raising his head proudly above that of the horse.

The Kingdom of Vaude had no Merlin. King Richard's father, King John had not been a believer in either science or magic. Truth be told, he hadn't been much of a believer in anything beyond food and drink; food and drink for himself. The extremely obese king had suffered a major heart attack and died on maneuvers with his knights when a bear had approached the sedan chair in which he was being carried. King John left his son, now King Richard of Vaude, and two daughters, Amy and Anne. Daughter Amy had married King Irv's son, Prince Sol and given birth to Irv's grandson, DI, who was the light of old Irv's life, along with his ginger tabby cat, Gaolbird.

Gaolbird, or Bird for short, had been rescued by the good king and his knights many years before from a drain in Berten on Cherwell where the local innkeeper had left the animal to drown, the man not being fond of cats. King Irv's rescue of the tiny feline and his subsequent words with the landlord of the Berten Arms had nearly caused an incident of bloodshed between the two kingdoms.

But that was all in the past. The knights of Warehouse Castle still avoided drinking at the Cherwell Arms pub, but the two monarchs had long ago buried the hatchet on this incident. Alas, there was still friction between the two as, at Prince Sol's urging, Richard of Vaude had built a Christian cathedral on the outskirts of his realm and lured Friar Agnello and his church away from Berten on Cherwell. The good Christian father had moved the religious seat of the area from Berten to Vaude in spite of the latter kingdom's close alliance with the Jewish kingdom of Wholesale.

So that was how things stood as the two Merlins set off toward the largest population center on their island accompanied by the knights and noblemen of two small British nations in a time before that island's history was even being formally recorded.

But there were legends of other great kings in these times. Who knew just what to believe? So it was with great anticipation that

Hershel set off with a small crew from the English Midlands for the far off city of Londres, a place they'd all heard tales about but had never seen.

Their little caravan was all a bubble with rumors and tales of who they might meet. One or two of King Bertie's knights confessed they were fearful about what they might find. They accepted Max, their king's magician, as a harmless enough character, but what if these so-called Merlins from other lands were into *black* magic? Or if, as some rumors had it, they could steal souls for the devil himself? Would they end up turned into goats or other farm beasts?

"I just wish our king had persuaded at least one of the novice priests to accompany us," Sir Vivian, one of King Bertie's men kept repeating. "I have a wife and small child that I must return to and protect. Fat lot of good I can do them if I'm turned into kind of some heathen animal."

Hershel chuckled softly to himself. What a superstitious lot these simple fellow were. Everyone with a brain knew a human couldn't be transformed into a goat, though at times he wished that he had the power to do just that to some of these loud mouthed folks from their neighboring kingdom.

# THREE

Their first day's travels brought them to Woburn Abbey where they were welcomed by the local monks. The friars were full of questions for Hershel as to how Ernesto and Julio, the local vintners of Wholesale Kingdom were doing with their new grapes from the future. No one paid much attention to the travelers from Berten on Cherwell.

How is it, King Bertie's knights wondered, that these good Christian brothers are more interested in talking to a Jewish magician than those of us from a much more pious land?

Finally, as they set up their encampment for the night, the monks came round to talk to the rest of the entourage, but it didn't make anyone feel much better, as the main topic of discussion was the large and wonderful new cathedral in the kingdom of Vaude. How pleased the Lord must be to have such a magnificent structure erected in his honor!

King Bertie's knights ended up drowning their sorrows in the free wine offered by the local brothers of Woburn Abbey. Being mainly beer drinkers, these men were not accustomed to the strong wine that the local abbot brewed. Max the Merlin and his entire group ended up very drunk, passing out along the abbey grounds even before the evening was fully dark.

Mounting up and heading out the next morning was a frightful scene. While King Irv's knights were up early, breakfasted on the bread and cheese the abbot of Woburn provided and ready to proceed on, Max and his men from Berten on Cherwell had all they could do to pull up their pants and stand on two legs. The abbot's proffered food sent these men rushing for the bushes where they lost much of what they'd consumed the night before. Mounting their horses provided a slapstick scene that could keep an audience in stitches for hours.

The sun was high in the spring sky by the time their group finally got onto King's Highway and headed in the proper southerly direction. King Bertie's knight, Sir Vivian, who had prophesized being turned into a goat, kept nodding his aching head and telling the others that the heathen process he feared had already begun, and they weren't even in the clutches of the largest group of these Godless magicians yet.

The procession moved more slowly than they should have, barely reaching the outskirts of St. Albans by nightfall thanks to the dragging of heels by King Bertie's lot. They camped outside the churchyard there, only a single priest coming out of the local parish to acknowledge them and wish them well. No one offered them wine or ale. Hershel had his own small firkin of ale, one of three or four, which he shared with the knights from King Irv's staff. They camped separately from the Cherwell bunch on either side of a small stream which seemed to be agreeable to both lots.

Sir Jakob, King Irv's senior knight on the journey, approached King Bertie's group to offer some bread and beans, but no one in the other camp seemed to have much of an appetite.

"All the more for our lot," Jakob chuckled as he returned to Hershel's camp, where they sang Jewish folk melodies and songs of victory about their kingdom.

King Irv and the Holy Grail

Everyone was in better spirits the next morning. Sir Vivian crossed the stream to ask Sir Jakob if they might have some of those beans on toasted bread to break their fast before they broke camp. King Irv's bunch were happy to share and everyone was mounted up and ready to roll shortly after sunrise.

They progressed well through the pass at Watford Junction and on south. They could smell the big city hours before they actually reached its outskirts. A combination of smoke and human waste seemed to fill the air as they progressed south.

By noontime, there were crude signs posted along the roadside telling them that the city and the Merlin's Convention was dead ahead. The smells grew stronger as they approached a sluggish body of water flowing in the direction that they were headed. They continued along the river's edge until they could see the smoke rising on the stream's other bank. Another two miles and they came upon a small, crude gate across the roadway and a man selling encampments for the Merlin's convention.

As there was no common currency across the island, the barker was accepting all manner of valuables in payment for space to set up encampments. Hershel offered a firkin of the Wholesale Kingdom's ale, which was readily accepted. He quickly turned to Max, the Cherwell Merlin to let him know that he now owed King Irv big-time.

The convention grounds were a wide plane of mud with a sort of theater construction at the center. The theater consisted of a large stage backed up against the river and wooden grandstands flanking it on two sides. A colorful canvas marquee festooned with advertising for local brewers, public houses and other businesses that catered to travelers capped the stage. Hershel noted that there was no one selling pizza. He'd heard rumors that some pilgrims had stolen the idea from Wholesale's Roadside Attraction but, apparently, the rumors had been wrong. Either that or the folks who had tried to copy Princess Judy's efforts hadn't gotten it right and had failed.

Directly opposite the stage, there was a large open area roped off where spectators could enter for a small price to stand in the field and view the proceedings. Hawkers walked through the crowd offering warm beer, meat pies and loaves of bread for sale.

Hershel was glad that he'd brought plenty of ale and food stuffs for the knights of King Irv's Wholesale Kingdom. From what he could see, these local people were asking far too much for what they were selling to the crowd, but then again, wasn't that what conventions were all about?

Just as soon as they'd pitched their tents, King Bertie's entourage was queued up for the ferry boat across the Thames to go and party in the capitol city. Hershel and King Irv's men had an ale or two from Hershel's private stock and decided to call it an early night. They could sit around a campfire and exchange tales of their various brave exploits. Tomorrow would be a full day of lectures and meetings.

 **FOUR**

The following morning, the program opened with a speech by a magician from Londres about how close they all were to turning base metals into gold. "I know were're just moments away from discovering how to accomplish this discovery," he told the assembled crowd, " and when we finally master this little feat, we, the magicians, will all be in control, holding our kings, lords and other overseers in the pockets of our robes.

"All it will take is for all of us assembled here to put our heads together and share the experiments we've made. By the time we leave this river bank later in the week, we'll have the key to unify the island on which we live for our own gain! We'll control the churches and the monarchs. No one will be able to stop us!"

Hershel chuckled to himself. If only it could be so easy. The Rabbi would just love this man's little speech. He knew from his own studies that gold could not be produced from lesser metals. All the chemical elements had their own special properties which couldn't be changed by magic or prayer. These Merlins were all wasting their time and efforts. Hopefully, his own address on time travel would hold some sway over them. At least travel across time had been proven as a factual entity, proven by himself. Forget about changing the chemical structure of one metal into another. He'd have his chance the next day to explain something much more crucial to them all.

This man's ideas about gold were echoed throughout the day by speaker after speaker, although none actually offered a formula for such a chemical transition. Everyone said it could, and would be done, but no one could say just how.

At the close of the day's presentations, Hershel sat sipping his ale, gazing at the stars overhead and woolgathering about how his words the following day might affect history. As he lay back in the tall grass with his eyes half closed, a tall, thin man in a blue conical hat covered with stars and crescents sat down quietly beside him. This newcomer also looked up toward the heavens but said nothing. Finally, becoming aware of his presence, Hershel spoke to the man.

"Can I offer you an ale from my King's land of Wholesale?"

"That would be quite jolly," the stranger answered, "and then we could talk a bit."

Hershel signaled for one of his fellows to fetch this stranger a pint of Wholesale ale. When the tankard was in the newcomer's hand, he said, "I'm Hershel, Merlin of the Wholesale Kingdom, a couple days' ride north of here. And you?"

"Sorry, old thing," the newcomer replied, "Didn't mean to be rude. Sten's the name. I'm Merlin to good King Arthur, out in the wild west, Tintagel, actually. I just received a strong vibe off of you, like we might be like-minded chaps. You're not one of these Christian types, are you?"

It was more a statement than a question and Hershel quickly replied.

"My kingdom is mostly Jewish, and you?"

"Druids, I'm afraid," Sten told him, "and taking a lot of flak from these Christian chaps of late. How about you?"

"We get along okay with our Christian neighbors," Hershel told him, "although one or two of them get on my wick from time to time. We regularly play golf with the Christian padre, I mean my king, my Rabbi and I."

"Rabbi?" Sten queried, "What's a Rabbi?"

"Well," Hershel answered, "He's kinda like our spiritual leader. He's the guy that guides us as to what's right and what's wrong, according to some very old scrolls he's studied we call the Torah."

"And what is this golf thing, then?" Sten asked.

"Well, that's a little bit harder to explain," Hershel told him with knitted brows. "It's a game that a friend of mine brought back to us from many years into the future. Do you believe in time travel?"

Sten chuckled. "Never gave it much thought, actually," he replied. "Though it doesn't seem to be out of the realm of possibilities, are you telling me that you've actually dome some of this travel across time?"

"Well, yeah," Hershel told the man. "That's what I intend to address this gathering about tomorrow. I've gone to the future many times and brought back some really cool stuff, like this game called golf. Also a tasty culinary dish called pizza and ale in small tin containers that you can carry around with you."

"Some pretty fanciful sounding stuff," Sten told Hershel. "I think my good King Arthur would like to meet with you and your good king. I can't wait to hear your presentation on the 'morrow.

"My King Arthur invented the 'round table,' a table that is round so everyone sitting at it is equal, like, no head of the table, so no one can feel superior to anyone else."

"Does that idea work?" Hershel asked with an open expression.

"In theory," Sten answered, "Yes, but in practice… Well, we've got a few big egos in our land that kinda defeat the purpose of the whole thing."

The two sat in silence for a long time, finishing two more tankards each before Sten turned and extended his hand to Hershel.

"It has been a great pleasure meeting you, my new friend. Perhaps you'll do me the honor of visiting my humble encampment at the close of festivities tomorrow? We're just to the right of the main stage under the red and green flag bearing the winged dragon, and I can repay your hospitality with some of our own Tintagel Ale."

 **FIVE**

On Saturday morning, the second day of the Merlin's Convention, Hershel opened the proceeding with his talk about time travel. In the first ten minutes of his lecture, at least a dozen small Christian kingdoms got up and walked out, some shouting hostile comments about God and the Lord's plan. Those that remained were paying rapt attention to Hershel's talk.

Sten sat in the first row, grinning and winking as Hershel spoke. A group that hailed from the far north, near Hadrian's wall, nodded agreement at each point in Hershel's talk, as though they might have experienced such phenomenon. Others just seemed to be fascinated by the idea that man could venture across time.

When the convention broke for a mid-day meal, some of the very Christian groups who'd walked out on Hershel's address were hastily packing up their camps and departing the proceedings, scattering cloves of garlic in their wake and waving large, wooden crosses. The event's promoters, not feeling one way or another about philosophical leanings, were sorry to see them go but, at the same time, glad they'd collected the fees from these groups up front.

The afternoon's program was suddenly turned away from producing gold from base metals and toward the idea that it might be possible to travel across time and space. The Christian kingdoms that remained were all a clamor with the idea that it might be possible to go back and shake hands with Jesus, their savior, or at least bear witness to his teachings and his subsequent crucifixion.

In small groups, Hershel tried to explain his globe and the method with which he was able to pinpoint a place to where he could go forward or backward across the ages, but the assembled masses wanted a simple solution. Nobody appeared interested in the science behind time travel.

Hershel turned down a dozen offers to leave King Irv's service and work for other rulers around the island.

"Hey," he told them, "I'm sort of retired. I drink ale and play golf with my liege, and occasionally I'll make a trip to the future. I don't want the responsibility of a regular gig, no matter what your kings might be paying. I got a good life and I'm stickin' to it!"

The assembled groups scratched their heads at the idea of golf as well as the concept of retirement. Didn't the Lord require one to work as long as he was able? How could one just 'stop working' and still be a good citizen? Wasn't idleness the devil's workshop?

As the sun set on the banks of the Thames, Hershel brought a couple of King Irv's knights to King Arthur's encampment under the Pendragon banner. Although some of Arthur's men seemed a bit skeptical, most were quite open minded. Hershel told about how he'd discovered that certain crystals could provide energy to power things, and how this power had led to his small tin vehicle that could, with the aid of his global map of the world, take him to distant lands in future times.

"And could this same energy take us back into the past?" Sten had inquired. "As in back to old Israel where we could prove once and for all if these Christian folks are either right or wrong? I only ask as King Arthur's good lady, Guinevere, seems to be obsessed with all this Christian nonsense."

"I've no doubt that it could," Hershel told him. "I believe that time and space are a kind of filing system, because we couldn't handle everything that's out there all at once."

This statement earned Hershel some confused looks, but no one wanted to contradict such a confident master, so no one raised questions or arguments.

In the end, when the remaining groups were folding their tents and getting ready to head home, it came down to just the small encampment from Berten on Cherwell and the Wholesale Kingdom remaining in the vast, muddy field with the knights of their so-called "round table" supporting Sten, the Merlin of King Arthur.

The soldiers and noblemen of these groups drank up the remains of the ale on offer and cleaned out the vendors of their various meats and pastries while Hershel and Sten discussed the possibilities of what time travel could do to benefit their two kings. With food and ale running low, the two groups bid each other farewell and headed back across the wild English countryside to their respective homes, pledging to meet again very soon in order to continue their discussion.

Hershel's head was all a swim as his small caravan traveled north toward the midlands. In Sten, he reasoned, he'd finally met his match, another Merlin as smart and as dedicated to science as himself. He said a silent prayer that this distant magician would actually contact him again, maybe even come to the Wholesale Kingdom to visit. There was so much wisdom they could share. He could even offer to take Sten in his time machine to visit the future England where King Irv's son-in-law, Rutherford, taught at an advanced university. It wasn't often that he met someone who was his own mental measure. So far, his liege, King Irv had been the closest he'd come to a true equal.

And on that note, what of Sten's monarch, King Arthur? From what his new friend had told him, this Arthur could also be another intellectual giant. Sten had said that the man was a Druid, a Pagan. Maybe Irv and Arthur could become great friends, even form a non-Christian alliance to unify their island as a place where all beliefs and faiths would be equally welcome.

Part Two
A Meeting of Like Minds

SIX

A number of uneventful months passed. Hershel had almost forgotten about the convention in Londres when one day a large complement of soldiers showed up at the gates of the Wholesale Castle. King Irv immediately summoned Hershel to his high battlements for advice on how to deal with this force. Although the gathering of mounted knights didn't appear hostile, King Irv wasn't sure what to expect. In his long rule, he'd never before been confronted with such a sizable entourage.

Hershel coaxed his king down the castle's broad stone steps through the portcullis and out to the forecourt, right by the ninth green, where they stepped forward to greet this large force of men. He immediately recognized Sten, the Merlin that served King Arthur.

"No worries, my liege," he told Irv, "I know these people. I met the Merlin of this group some months ago at our Merlin's convention in Londres. I believe they come in peace."

"That is exactly what we do," proclaimed a tall and muscled man in a neat armored breastplate at the front of the group. He removed his helmet to reveal a head of thick red curls and a neatly trimmed beard of the same color.

The red headed stranger nudged his steed forward, his hand extended down from his tall place in the saddle. "I am Arthur, the King of Tintagel and the land known as Cornwall. We come in peace at the invitation of your good Merlin, Hershel." The horseman nodded his head toward Hershel. "I have been told that your man has discovered a way to travel across time and I would be in your service to learn more about this sort of magic."

King Irv shot a look at Hershel that told him he wasn't sure if he should be angry or pleased.

"Yes, highness," Hershel told Irv, standing at stiff attention just for show. "I did meet with King Arthur's man, Sten, at the convention some months ago and invited them here to meet with you and your good knights. I figured it wouldn't hurt to share our little secret."

King Irv's face broke into a broad smile. "Well, if Hershel says you're alright, that's good enough for me. Shalom and mahzel! Please, dismount and follow me through the gates to my broad bailey. Can I offer you ale or would you prefer our own special California Cabernet wine?"

"Cabernet wine?" King Arthur questioned as he swung down from his mount. "I've heard of wine, either red or white in color, but what means this Cabernet?"

King Irv gave forth with a hearty laugh. "It's a special grape that my Merlin brought to me from the future. I think you'll be impressed."

King Arthur smiled. "Will these surprises never cease," he purred. "May my knights set up a camp here before your castle?" he inquired, gesturing toward the broad lawn near the highway, which drew a frown from Irv.

"Oh, no, no," the King barked with a serious face. That's right in the middle of my eighteenth fairway. That would never do."

"Eighteenth fairway," Arthur asked with a puzzled look. "What is an eighteenth fairway? I see nothing there but a broad, green expanse of lawn?"

"It has to do with the game of golf," Hershel put in. "That's where we finish up our game so it can't be blocked."

Arthur's face became more puzzled, even a little distressed. "Are we welcome here or not?" he barked.

"Oh, you are most welcome here, my good king, but I have a much nicer place in mind for your men to set up their tents. It's our festival grounds, just up the highway by that field you passed with the large stones, up by where you might have seen our wine bar and roadside attraction. You, sir, shall be given accommodations in Warehouse Castle. We have a very cozy suite of guest rooms. And later, after you've settled in, I show you our little game we call golf."

King Arthur turned and motioned towards his troops with his right hand. As he did so, a slender lady with long cascading blond hair came forward, riding side-saddle on a milk white mare.

"This is my lady, Queen Guinevere." Arthur nodded again, and Sten the Merlin approached on a dappled gray gelding. "And this is my Merlin, Sten. Do you also have a room for Sten? I like to keep him close at hand."

"But of course," Irv told the monarch. "I feel the same way about Hershel, my own man of magic. Let me dispatch one of my knights to show your entourage to the festival ground where they can pitch their marquees while you and your fair queen come inside to meet my wife, Queen Sophie."

SEVEN

Once settled in Warehouse Castle's formal lounge, glasses of Cabernet in the hands of King Arthur, Queen Guinevere and the king's two top knights, King Irv introduced them all to Queen Sophie, his grandson, Prince D I, and Gaolbird, the royal cat. 'Bird' took an instant liking to Arthur licking the man's hand and hopping into his lap, which right away told Irv that he could trust this stranger.

"So you're interested in time travel?" King Irv asked as a conversation starter.

"Most assuredly so," replied his red-headed guest. "Firstly, because we are always curious about science and the world that surrounds us, and beyond that, because we are constantly being besieged by the kingdoms around us who are increasingly turning to these crazy Roman Christian beliefs."

"Ah, yes," Irv told the man. "We've had some problems with this lot ourselves… But our Rabbi gets along well the Roman friar who runs the Christian church in our neighboring kingdom. Friar Agnello plays golf with me and our Rabbi once or twice a week."

"Golf," Arthur barked with an inquisitive continence. "There's that term again. What is this golf? I've not heard such a word or of such a game before. Please tell me all."

"Tell you," Hershel laughed, "how about we show you."

"Hershel, please," Irv chuckled loudly. "Some explanation might be in order first.

"Arthur my new friend, Hershel, in his travels across time met a man in the future. This man introduced Hershel to many new ideas, such as ale that can be distributed and sipped from pint sized metal vessels. This man in the future also showed Hershel a game that is very popular in advanced times. It involves hitting a small ball with various assortments of clubs with the aim of finally knocking this small ball into a tiny hole in the grass. Am I saying this right, Hershel?" the king asked.

"Not bad for starters," Hershel laughed. "Of course my king has dreadfully oversimplified the game, but it should help you get the idea."

"This sounds an interesting challenge," King Arthur told them, nodding to his knights. "So are we to try and learn this game while we are your guests?" he asked.

"But of course," Irv told his visitors. "Just let me see what kind of clubs I can rustle up to fit each of you."

"Clubs to fit?" Arthur inquired. "This game requires a special club?"

"About twelve of them, actually," King Irv told his guest. "Each with its head angled at a different pitch to lengthen the arc of the ball when you hit it… But that's more information than you need to get started."

"This does have my curiosity at a high pique," King Arthur mused. "Clubs with heads on them? And you have such clubs that we may borrow?"

"But of course," King Irv told them. "We want to give you every advantage so that you might win in this game."

Queen Guinevere giggled and almost choked on a sip of wine. "My Arthur does like to win," she snorted. "Does your good lady also play this golf game?"

"No," Hershel quickly put in, "it's a guy thing." That earned him a cross look from Queen Sophie.

"So what do you think of my Cabernet wine?" Sophie asked her guests to change the subject. "Hershel also brought this wine back from the future, so much classier than drinking *ale* out of tin vessels."

"And what would be this ale that comes in tin, by the way?" asked one of Arthur's knights.

"I'm sure we'll get to try this in due time, Lancelot," Arthur told his man.

King Irv called Wendy over, one of the castle's serving wenches, and whispered something softly to her. Wendy left the room and returned moments later with four pint cans of Mann's Strong Ale. She ripped the first can from the web of plastic bonding the cans together, popped the pull-tab top and handed it to King Arthur with a clumsy curtsey, balancing the other cans that were still held together by the plastic.

King Arthur took a hesitant sip, smiled, and tipped his head back for a full draught. "That is good!" he exclaimed with a loud belch. "So how does such good ale get into these small tubes of tin?"

"They've got these big machines in the future," Hershel told Arthur. The machines force the ale into the little tubes and then seal them shut. The future is the only place we can get this stuff, so we kinda save it for special occasions. But our Wholesale Kingdom brews some pretty tasty ale of our own, which I hope you will get to sample soon."

Seeing that the guest king was pleased, Wendy passed the remaining cans around to the other of Arthur's knights who were present. Irv, Sophie and Guinevere continued to sip their Cabernet wine.

"So what other treasures does the future hold?" King Arthur asked, tossing down his empty ale can and extending his hand toward Wendy for the one remaining can.

"Well," Hershel told him with a wink, "They have carriages that move forward without any horses or oxen to pull them. They call them 'motor cars,' and they have other carriages that fly men through the sky like giant birds. And small glass balls that glow with sufficient brightness to light up a room."

"Amazing!" the guest king sputtered, "What magic there is out in the world that we've yet to discover."

"And they have a very tasty food in the future they call pizza," Queen Sophie added with a proud look. "My daughter, Princess Judith, figured out the secrets and became very good at preparing pizza, didn't she Irv?"

"Pizza," Sir Lancelot repeated with a questioning look. "I've never heard of this pizza."

"Like I said," Queen Sophie grinned smugly, "It comes from the future."

"And our daughter does make an excellent pizza," Irv, the proud father, emphasized.

"And when do we get to meet your fine daughter the princess?" asked Queen Guinevere, leaning forward in her chair.

"Well, I'm afraid you can't," King Irv told them sadly. "Princess Judith fell in love with a man from the future and went there to live with him."

King Arthur's jaw dropped to his leather-plated chest. "You have a daughter who *lives* in these future times? How can that be?"

"Yeah, it surprised us," Irv chuckled. "Hershel, my Merlin, brought this guy back in his time machine, a clever guy with skin as brown as a little nut. Next thing we know, Judith is cookin' special meals for the guy and acting all moony around him. So Hershel took her to the future to see where this guy, Rutherford is his name, where he lives and, next thing you know, Judith is asking if she can marry the man."

"And you gave your consent?" Guinevere asked with wide eyes. "To marry someone not of your own kingdom, who, as you described him, had skin 'as brown as a nut'? How could this be?"

"Oy, who can ever understand love," Queen Sophie sighed wistfully, rolling her eyes.

"Hey," Hershel interjected, "if you want to try pizza, that little roadside attraction up by where your lot is camping serves a really good pizza. And they have some remarkable wines for sale there also. Princess Judith actually started the place, but when she went to the future her friend Debbie took it over. If you like curiosities, we even have a tame dragon there that you can look at right up close."

"A *tame* dragon," Sir Lancelot remarked. "I've never heard of such a thing."

"Smokey ain't our first tame dragon," Hershel told him with enthusiasm. "Smokey's mother, Burnie, was our first dragon. King Irv brought her here, but that's another story."

"This Wholesale Kingdom is a remarkable place," King Arthur said in a subdued voice. "I'm so thankful that my Merlin ran into your Merlin. I feel there is so much I can learn here, over and above your game of golf."

# EIGHT

Tuesday morning found King Arthur and King Irv standing on the first tee of the Warehouse Castle golf course, accompanied by Hershel and Rabbi Weiss.

"This is a fairly long hole," Irv instructed his guest after making his own shot as a demonstration. "You'll probably want to use your number two wooden club, what we call a 'driver' to get this one. First, you need to stand with your legs apart and address the ball..."

"You mean I need to speak to it?" King Arthur asked, sounding a bit confused.

"Oh, no, no," Hershel cut in. "By address the ball, Irv means you have to line it up with your club so you can whack it straight down between the trees to where that little red flag is waving over yonder, that's where the first hole is."

King Arthur nodded agreement although he didn't have a clue what they were talking about. He drew his driver back over his shoulder, closed his eyes and gave the little white ball a resounding whack as he'd seen Irv do before him. He reopened his eyes when he heard applause from Irv, Hershel and the Rabbi.

"Right down the middle," Rabbi Weiss sang. "Are you sure you haven't played golf before?"

King Arthur smiled as he stepped aside. Hershel, a bit unsettled by Arthur's good start, sliced his ball onto the edge of the rough, but not too far from the green. The good Rabbi got close to the green dead center in the fairway near where Irv's ball had landed.

On the green, King Arthur putted his ball in for a birdie. Irv wrote this off as beginner's luck as he took two extra strokes to sink his ball. Irv was now two strokes behind both his Merlin and his Rabbi, and three shots behind his so-called student.

King Arthur proved to be a quick study, but was still beaten by the three experienced golfers. "I must teach my knights this game," he told King Irv over tankards of ale outside Hershel's cave after the match. "This has proven a most relaxing and enjoyable afternoon."

Sten, King Arthur's Merlin, joined them at Hershel's place and asked if they might go inside to see the laboratory where the man of magic worked. Hershel was very pleased with their interest and swept his hand along in a 'please enter' motion. The guest king glanced around Hershel's small lab, commenting on various pieces of equipment. He bent over for a closer look at the Merlin's globe, then gave it a spin. "And what is the significance of this interesting and colorful ball?"

"That is a map of our world," Irv stated proudly, showing that he was no dummy when it came to science.

"Map of our world?" Arthur chuckled. "But look around you, my good fellow. Our world is flat, as flat as a table top."

Hershel laughed. "I know it *appears* to be flat, your highness, but believe me, it ain't. If it was, I wouldn't be able to travel through time. See, the world is round and it's always spinning very fast, which holds us down so we don't fall off. I use this ball, what we call a globe, to direct my travels from place to place in time."

"Most improbable," Sten put in, "but you *could* be right. I'll have to give this some deep thought."

Hershel stepped over to King Arthur's side and pointed to the globe's surface. "You see this blob of green at the edge of this big patch of blue? That's the island we're living on. And here," he drew his finger to the side of England on the map, "is Wholesale Kingdom, where we're standing now." He moved his finger slightly down the ball's surface. "And here in Londres, where you and I met, Sten," he said casting his eyes towards his fellow man of magic.

Hershel then traced a line west along the island. "And this is where you live, I believe. If you can read the tiny writing on the surface of this sphere, I believe it says Cornwall."

"Extraordinary," exclaimed King Arthur, "if it's true."

"I'd bet my life on its veracity," Hershel told him with an affirmative nod. Arthur looked him up and down while Sten stood with his arms folded across his chest.

The group sat out front in contemplative silence for some time, sipping ale in a meditative sort of way. Finally, King Arthur spoke. "I can see we can learn a lot from your people, King Irv. The Gods must have arranged this meeting. I'm pleased that I consented to send Sten to Londres for that gathering and even more so that I've had this opportunity to meet with you both." He thought for another minute and then added, "And I'm very intrigued with this golf game you're teaching me. Life is a remarkable adventure, is it not?"

🐉 NINE 🐉

That evening, King Irv and Queen Sophie invited Arthur and Guinevere to join them in a trip to Vaudeville, the seat of the next kingdom to the east.

"We have an alliance with King Richard of Vaude," Irv told his guests. "They are a Christian kingdom, but they are happy to live in peace with us. My own son, Prince Sol, is best friends with the monarch of Vaude. He's actually married to this king's sister. And they have a great theater there. You'll enjoy the cabaret!" he assured them.

Morrie the Jester was headlining the bill that evening, along with a popular dance company and a collection of musicians that included some alumni from King Irv's own Roadside Attraction.

As the curtain rose and Morrie took the stage, Hershel told everyone, "You'll love this guy. He's such a card!"

"So, you know what you call a court Jester without a lady friend?" Morrie asked the crowd.

"Homeless," he cackled.

"And the Court Jester who won big in the horse races? His monarch asked 'what are you gonna do with all that money?' He said, 'I'm gonna keep doing my schtick until it's all gone.' How about that? Morrie slapped his knees and broke up in laughter at his own lines.

"And I hear we have some guests in the house tonight," he continued, pulling himself together, but just barely, "from the far west of our little island. Welcome King Arthur and Queen Guinevere. You must be a real putz to come here looking for support. Here in Vaude, we used to be known for having the fattest and laziest king in all the realm. But we're getting better now. Now we have a Jew for a neighbor and his son's best friend for a ruler, oy vey, whatever that means.

"Hey, I love you, King Irv. Just keep our little secret, nobody knows I'm Jewish too," Morrie delivered with a nervous laugh.

"And this man is funny?" King Arthur asked Irv.

"This isn't one of his better nights," King Irv replied sourly. "I hope you'll enjoy the dancers and the music."

"So do I," Arthur replied with a serious face.

Hershel shrugged his shoulder and gave a sort of 'what-do-I-know' look.

After the show, when King Arthur had consumed uncounted pints of ale, Morrie came out to apologize.

"I'm sorry, your highness, if I said anything that might have offended you."

A rather squiffy Arthur thought for a minute, then replied, "I'm not from around here, so I might have been a bit over sensitive. If you ever make a tour of the west, maybe you can stop at Tintagel Castle and entertain some of my friends."

Morrie's face brightened instantly. "I'd love that, your highness. Listen, I've got this great routine about people with gas in an old folk's home."

"That sounds fascinating," Arthur told him. "I'll keep your name on file." With that, the guest king turned back to his drink, dismissing the Vaudeville funnyman. Morrie gave his shoulders a theatrical shrug and exited stage left.

"Well, I guess we can't have everything," Irv apologized. "Usually, the man is funnier than this. Maybe he *is* just having a bad night."

"I'm not that big on comedy myself," Arthur told him. "I prefer contests of sport and skill. Now to see my knights in mock battles, *that's* entertainment."

Irv made a mental note that he and his new friend were not quite alike in their thinking, then returned to the conversation. "So what did you think of the Morris Dancers?"

"I thought they were fabulous," Queen Guinevere loudly proclaimed. "I just love dancing. If only my big lug of a husband would take me dancing sometime," she added with daggered eyes at King Arthur. "Now Lancelot, he's a great dancer. He's got the moves." King Arthur made a dour face and tossed back the rest of his drink.

"Sometimes I wonder if I can trust my own closest friends," he mumbled into his tankard.

On returning to Warehouse Castle, Arthur and Guinevere went straight up to their rooms. Queen Sophie gave Irv a scolding look and followed their guests upstairs. King Irv called for another pint of ale and sat on one of the divans in the castle's main hall where he was joined by his cat, Bird.

"Bird, my old maugy," he told the animal, stroking the feline's soft orange fur. "Sometimes I don't know if I was cut out to be a ruler of men. It could be so much simpler if I just brewed beer or planted crops...

"Ah, but then I probably wouldn't have these wonderful hours to spend talking with you, my little friend."

At that, Irv picked up a stray piece of string from the floor and began to wave it back and forth before his furry buddy. Bird's eyes followed the strand while his tail fluttered almost in time with the bit of thread. After a minute, Bird attacked the string, caught it in his mouth and pulled back. After a short tussle, Irv jerked the string upward and Bird followed it, landing in the king's lap. King Irv quickly scooped his pet into his arms and they started butting heads. The pair ended up in a kitty love feast, Bird purring loudly while the king softly stroked the cat's belly.

Queen Sophie found the two snuggled together on the divan in the early hours when she came to check why her husband had not made it up to bed. "Irv," she scolded, "you and that cat. So do you want to come up to bed with me now or would you prefer to just stay here with your pet?"

Reluctantly, King Irv kissed his feline pal goodnight and followed his queen up to their bed chambers. Tomorrow would be another long day of entertaining guests.

TEN

Over a good old English fry up of eggs, baked beans, tomatoes and mushrooms the next morning, King Irv met once again with his guests. Arthur seemed a little anxious and, after a few forkfuls of food, looked Irv right in the eye.

"We've played your game of golf," he began. "We've sampled ale and wine from the future and we've even sampled this far away dish called pizza. But my Merlin and I came here to learn about travel across time. So far you've talked around it, shown us a round ball of a map supposed to represent our world, but you shared arse-all about how you are able to travel through time. I think it's time we got serious about this time travel thing. Will your Merlin show us how it is done or not?"

"My apologies," King Irv gave them with a hurt face. "We don't mean to hide anything. We've just never thought of time travel as such an important idea. Hershel, old thing, can you take some time this morning and talk with our guests about how we're able to travel across time?"

"Ah, well, sure, Irv," Hershel said, looking up from his breakfast. "Time travel? No big thing. But first you've got to understand the crystals that provide the power for the time machine and some of the other science behind it."

Both Sten and Arthur bore their eyes into Hershel as he spoke. "Do we really need all the background?" King Arthur asked. "Can we not just partner with you, share some of our riches with your kingdom and ride with you to these places in time?"

"Well, there's only room for two in my time thingy. I mean I can't carry a whole bunch of people. And where is it in time you wish me to take you?" Hershel asked.

There was a bit of hemming, ahhing and throat clearing before Arthur finally spoke. "We've been led to understand that these Christians who plague us are all in a dither to find something they call a '**Holy Grail**.' They say it's a cup or bowl that their so-called savior, this Jesus fellow, drank from at his last supper before the Roman's murdered him."

"Or maybe it's a cup that caught some of this Jesus fellow's blood while he was being murdered," Sten put in. "We're not sure, but if we can possess this cup or bowl, we'll have a bit of leverage on these Christian usurpers. That would be a big help to us."

"Our Christian neighbors don't pose any threat to us," King Irv smiled. "We get along quite nicely."

King Arthur leaned in very close, almost nose to nose with Irv. "My good queen, Guinevere, has been mesmerized by these Christian fellows. I believe my best knight, Lancelot, is telling her that he is also enamored of this Christian faith in a move to lure her to his bed. It may require all the evidence I can muster to retain my queen and save my marriage. So can we get to this time travel wheeze as quickly as possible, before my good knight has the chance to bed my good lady?"

King Irv was floored back into his throne. "My Merlin can save your kingdom?" he asked. "That puts a totally different spin on things. We will do all we can to help you! My God, what would Rabbi Weiss say to this?"

"So, what is this Jewish thing?" King Arthur asked. "We born of this island have always worshiped an earth-mother, a goddess who is mother and protector of us all. We see the Pendragon as the representative of our God." Arthur rolled up the sleeves of his tunic to reveal tattooed dragons encircling both his wrists. "This is our Pendragon," he proudly proclaimed. It was the very same dragon image that King Arthur's men had depicted on their battle flags.

King Irv and his Merlin's eyes met. Had Moses known of these far off people when he climbed that mountain long ago? If so, there was nothing they could remember of it in the Torah, but then their little island was a long way from Egypt, so maybe Moses hadn't thought of England as being all that important.

ELEVEN

As the breakfast dishes were cleared, King Irv asked, "Have these Christian fellows threatened you in any other way, I mean besides this one knight of yours who appears to lust after your good queen?"

"Actually, they have," Arthur barked emphatically. "There is this crazy Irish monk who calls himself Patrick. This man is obsessed with destroying my royal line, the House of Pendragon.

"Patrick seems driven to find this cup or bowl he refers to as 'the Holy Grail,' from which he believes his *'savior,'* Jesus, drank wine before he was murdered by Roman and Jewish savages, his words, not mine. This crazy monk goes on and on about forming a ginormous army to sail off to what he calls 'the Holy Land,' capture this grail and then murder as many of the un-Christian native of the place as he can. I must locate this Grail thing so I might use it to leverage better treatment of our Pagan people by all these crazy Christian folks, as well as stopping a huge loss-of-life in this far off land. And this Patrick has the gall to refer to my 'Pendragon' people as 'snakes!'"

"That does seem rather rude," King Irv agreed with a positive nod. "Is this man one of the Romans who invaded our lands?"

"That's the scary thing," Sten piped up. "He is an Irish *native*. I don't think he's ever been off the Emerald Island, apart from visiting us. These Irish! It's so easy to sell them a bill of goods as I believe the Romans did with our Patrick."

King Irv pondered these thought for a few moments until Hershel interrupted his meditation. "Ah, highness?" he queried, "Aren't these Irish folks supposed to be Pagans as well?"

"They always have been," thundered King Arthur, "until very recently. Now this Christian thing seems to be sweeping their island like a plague. I just don't understand it. And if you think these Christians hate us Pagans, I can tell you that they, at least the ones in Ireland, *really* dislike you Jews. They think you had something to do with killing their precious savior."

At this point, even though it was still early in the day, King Irv called for a round of ale to lubricate their thinking processes.

After a couple tankards of ale, Arthur gazed wistfully off into the sky and said, "This 'Grail' thing, I really believe that it's a stone vessel that the pagan Gods sent down to honor the Mother Sun God far back in the history of the Pendragon people, which is our own heritage. These Christians probably just stole the idea for their own, just like they stole our Winter Solstice and called it Christmas.

"Christmas?" Irv mused. "We don't do Christmas."

And with that, the small group fell into a contemplative silence.

After another round of drinks, Hershel volunteered, "So, you want to know more about time travel? Why don't we move this little meeting down to my cave and I'll try to explain what I can. I don't really know how I'm doing some of this myself. It's just like the spirit speaks to me and I follow what this little voice in my head says to do."

The small group of men walked from the castle across the second fairway to the Merlin's digs, where they all found stumps, rocks or stools to perch on in a circle. Hershel rummaged around for a minute or two, coming up with his original crystal solar panel.

"This is where it all began," he told his audience. "I discovered that if I attach metal wires to this box of quartz, it creates a power, and if I harness the power from these wires, it can do certain other things for me, like powering this tin egg…" Hershel turned with a hand extended like a game show model to point at his machine that had so often taken him through the eons.

King Arthur and his Merlin, Sten, were fidgeting in their seats, unsure where this strange lecture was going.

"This tin egg, "King Arthur parroted. "You mean that pile of metal dross behind you?"

"Exactly," Hershel answered. "You were expecting a coach with six white horses? Hey, it may not *look* like much, but it gets the job done, alright?"

The Cornish king gave Hershel a hurt look. "If you say so, sir, you are the magician."

"And a damn good one at that," Irv tossed in.

"So, anyway," Hershel told them, motioning everyone closer to his contraption. "This panel of quartz crystals on the top provides the power." He ran his hand across the machine's roof, then pointed to the thing's dashboard. "This little dial sets how far backward or forward I want to go in time. It's not really perfected as I'm not sure how to calibrate the age of our planet. According to the Torah, our world is just over four thousand years old, but so far it's been pretty accurate for wherever I've wanted to go."

Sten leaned in to give the dial a close inspection. "And how far in the past have you been able to travel?" he asked.

"Well, actually," Hershel told him, "I haven't had any reason to go back to the past. I've only gone forward, into the future. We were concerned about how our kingdom might fair when we were dead and gone."

"But you can go backwards as well?" Sten persisted.

"Well of course," Hershel blustered. "It's a time machine, ain't it?"

"This Holy Grail thing," King Arthur put in, "it would be something like five or six hundred years in the past, if these Christians are at all accurate in their measure of time. That's where we'd need to go."

"Oh yeah, right," Hershel replied sarcastically. "And if I could do this, what's in it for me?"

King Arthur and his Merlin looked at each other. Hershel did have a point. This Patrick fellow wasn't threatening the Wholesale Kingdom.

"We will pay you in gold bars," Arthur finally decided out loud. "I must have this grail thing at any cost."

🐉 TWELVE 🐉

After half a day of discussion, some of it over another round of golf, it was decided that Hershel would take Sten into the future, a run Hershel was familiar with, to get Arthur's man more familiar with time travel. When Sten could report back on the experience to his monarch, they would decide on a further course of action.

"We've got friends in this future place," Hershel told Sten, "business partners already. King Irv's son-in-law, Rutherford. He invested in a brewery way out in another time. It's in a place called San Francisco, in a land called California. You'll get a kick outta this place," Hershel assured Sten. "It's totally crazy."

Sten and Arthur gave each other questioning looks. Did Sten really want to go to someplace that was totally crazy? They knew nothing of this future, they only wanted to go to a specific point in the past.

"Have you actually done this time travel thing?" Arthur asked King Irv.

"Only once," Irv admitted. "And I'm not likely to ever try it again."

"But your daughter lives somewhere in this future place," Arthur reminded him.

"Well, yeah," King Irv admitted. "And my good queen Sophie goes there quite often, but I really didn't enjoy the one time I tried going there."

"And that was because..."

"It would take too long to explain," Irv told Arthur. "I went to this San Francisco place, not to where my daughter lives. Suffice it to say that it was just a bit too weird for me. I'd rather stay right here in Wholesale, drink ale, play golf and enjoy the company of my wife and my cat."

Arthur nodded his head in the affirmative although his wasn't sure he understood anything of what this crazy Jewish king had just told him.

"It is a very different world," King Irv continued, "Nothing like our little island. There are just so many people, lots more people than even in the densest areas of Londres, and all these horseless carriages everywhere."

"Hershel had mentioned something about these horseless carriages," Sten replied.

"And being neither a man of science nor a magician," King Arthur chuckled, patting Irv's sleeve, "I'm sure I would have felt much the same. So now, can we dispatch our Merlins to this future place and get this process started?"

Hershel finally agreed that they would depart the next morning, right after breakfast. "A man can't time travel on an empty stomach," he'd told Sten and Arthur with a wry grin, although he'd done it often enough. Hershel was, in fact, stalling while he put together a plan.

Ralph, the manager of their future brewery, would not be expecting a visit any time soon. Ralph was the computer nerd who had brought troops back through time some years before to attack

Warehouse Castle when Hershel had stolen grapes from Ralph's parent's vineyards in the future land of Napa Valley, California. Ralph's motley band of future warriors had been soundly defeated by the armies of King Irv and his neighboring ruler, King David of Vaude. Later, Hershel had brokered a deal between Ralph and King Irv's son-in-law, Rutherford, to finance a San Francisco brewery for Ralph in exchange for Ralph's surrendering the time travel software that he possessed.

The deal had made both Ralph and the Wholesale Kingdom millions of pounds over the ensuing years, not to mention Rutherford and Princess Judith's commissions on the arrangement. It had proved a most profitable venture for all involved. In fact, Ralph had only recently been brokering a deal to can the various ales he was brewing and sell them internationally. King Irv grinned widely at the thought, tins of ale from a future brewery that he himself owned a stake in. It had only been a scant five years earlier that he'd discovered this California place while trying to procure those special wine grapes that his queen had desired.

Before they got in Hershel's contraption, the Merlin produced an old carpetbag suitcase, from which he extracted some Levis blue jeans and a couple of Hawaiian shirts. "I think these should be about your size," he told Sten. "Try them on. If we're going to fit in at this future place, we have to be dressed like future people."

Sten gave a disdainful look at the bright red shirt Hershel handed him with the pattern of half naked girls in grass skirts. Was he sure this was how people in the future dressed? What a strange place this must be.

Hershel himself had donned the other, a bright blue thing with strangely leaved trees and jumping fish. The blue jeans Hershel told him to put on seemed frightfully confining to his manhood compared to the loose draw-string trousers Sten was used to.

THIRTEEN

S ten and Hershel materialized in the parking lot of Ralph's Metaphysical Brewing Company in Berkeley, California, in the year 2002 by the current Christian calendar. This time, Hershel had given more study to what would fit into the surroundings, so his time travel egg was now cloaked in the disguise of an Infinity Q-45 sport utility vehicle.

Sten exited the contraption with wide, almost scared eyes. A group of drunken Cal Berkeley students were coming out of the brewery, stumbling and laughing. A homeless man in a plastic poncho was sleeping against the wall of the next building, off to their left. On the curb, only ten feet away, a drunk stumbled with his black plastic bag containing a cheap bottle of wine.

"Are you sure we're in the right place?" Sten queried in a timid voice.

""Yeah," Hershel chuckled. "Welcome to San Francisco. That's the thing about time travel," he told his friend. "You never know quite what to expect. Just follow me, you'll feel more comfortable once we get inside the brewery."

They walked in the back door from the parking lot, passing the restrooms and the kitchen and entering the main bar area. Ralph was there and immediately recognized Hershel, coming forward to throw his arms around him in a giant bear hug.

"Hershel, my old friend," he gushed. "So good to see you! What brings you to the future?"

"Ah, Ralph?" Hershel said hesitantly, "I want you to meet someone from history. You ever read any of the legends of King Arthur of the Round Table? Well this here is King Arthur's Merlin, Sten, you know, like from the Sword and the Stone?"

Ralph burst into raucous laughter. "You gotta be kidding me, Hersh, for real?"

"Real as it gets," Hershel told him with a lopsided grin.

Sten didn't know what to say. He finally gave a hesitant," Sword and the Stone? What does that mean?"

"Well," Hershel told him. "Here in the future, your King Arthur is a kind of a cult figure, you understand cult figure? Yeah, probably not, he's like a hero. Someone they tell all these stories about. They even made a movie or two about him. What can I say? King Arthur is a big man in history."

"A movie?" Sten choked, "what's a movie?"

"Too difficult to explain right now," Hershel chuckled. "I'll take you to see one some time."

And with that, a small mob of young people started forming around the trio. "King Arthur? Cool!" and similar phrases abounded.

Ralph called some of his staff to their aid and they quickly spirited Hershel and Sten up a flight of stairs and into a private room reserved for special events and tastings.

"This is too cool," Ralph said when they were in the quiet protected space. "Hershel, you never cease to amaze."

"Th-th-this has to be the ba-ba-biggest pub I've ever seen," Sten stuttered.

"Like I said, welcome to the future," Hershel laughed, "And you ain't seen nothin' yet. Tomorrow, I'll show you the Golden Gate Bridge."

"Golden Gate Bridge," Sten parroted, "what's that?"

"Probably the biggest *bridge* you've ever seen," chuckled Ralph. "But for right now, would you like to sample my Berkeley Bitter? It's my personal favorite of the ales we have here."

"You brew more than one type of ale," Sten marveled. "Is there really a need for that?"

"We've got a dozen different varieties of beers and ales," Ralph proudly told him, "From German style lagers to India Pale Ales."

"German style? India ales," Sten repeated with a face full of confusion. "Around Cornwall and the west of our island we have only bitter ale. Nobody has ever asked for anything different. Oh, it may vary a bit in taste from one batch to the next, but it's still all just ale, isn't it?"

"Again, welcome to the future," Hershel repeated with a wide grin. Then turning to Ralph, he said, "Why don't you order up one of those little flight board things for our friend here, with the five small sample glasses? You can probably just select from the IPA's and other bitter ales. I don't think someone from our past would care for any light beers or lagers."

"How about I throw in one of our imperial stouts?" Ralph questioned with a mischievous grin.

"Yeah, that would probably work," Hershel answered.

Two flights of samples and two pints later, one of Berkeley Bitter and one of extra strong Big Bay IPA, Sten was grinning ear-to-ear and talking rather loudly. "This future place is alright," he hollered, slamming his pint glass down on the table. "Do you want to take me to that damn big bridge now?"

"Ah, I think we'll put that off until tomorrow, Sten," Hershel told him. "For right now, I think we should get you something to eat and then figure out where we can spend the night."

"I can get you a room at Motel 8, just a few blocks over," Ralph volunteered. "And I'll have one of the staff drive you there."

"That sounds good," Hershel told him. "But first, do you think Sten would like one of your Knob Hill Burgers? You know, the one with the two big patties and three different cheeses plus those little green chili peppers? I could sure use one of those about now, and lots of those French Fried Potatoes."

"Burgers?" Sten mumbled, "What is this burgers?"

"Future food," Ralph told him. "You'll like it."

When the large platters were set down before them, Hershel had to demonstrate how to add ketchup then place the top of the roll over the meat to close the sandwich. He picked up his own Knob Hill Burger in both hands and took a big bite as an example.

Sten's beef paddies slid around a bit when he gripped the sandwich, but after a mouthful or two, he got the hang of it. "Arthur and the knights would love this." he shouted a bit loudly. "This bread stuff keeps your hands from getting so smeared with fat. How did you ever think of such a thing?"

"Actually," Ralph told him, "it was another Englishman from our little island, the fifth earl of Sandwich, but that's another place in time. You don't want to go there now."

FOURTEEN

T he next morning was a Tuesday in San Francisco. The outside temperature was nearly eighty degrees, what might be
considered a heat wave in old England. Ralph had phoned
the rental car people the previous evening and Hershel and Sten
came down from their second floor room at Motel 8 to find a small
blue Fiat awaiting them in the hostelry's driveway. The desk clerk
handed them the keys as he held his hand out for a tip. All Hershel
had in his pocket were some pound notes from his last trip to Oxford in England. The hotel man gave the five pound note a strange
look, but accepted it without comment. He'd probably be able to
change it somewhere. California hotels were used to receiving for-
eign currency.

Hershel led his friend back inside where they ate bagels and
cream cheese from the breakfast bar, along with some pieces of
fruit and cups of tea.

"Just like time travel," Hershel told his friend, "one shouldn't
start a drive around the future on an empty stomach." Sten only
nodded and sipped something called Happy Hibiscus Tea. He
made a rude face at the taste of the brew. If this was tea in the future, they could keep it.

After their breakfast, Hershel handed Sten into the passenger
door of the small Italian car in the motel lot and showed him how
to plug in his seat belt. Hershel punched on the air conditioning
and they drove out onto University Avenue then turned onto San
Pablo, headed for the San Francisco Bay Bridge and the big city

itself. As they cleared the toll booth and pulled up the ramp, Sten's jaw dropped to his chest. "You're right, I've never seen a bridge so large," he marveled.

Hershel laughed loudly. "We ain't even near the Golden Gate yet. This is just a little warm-up bridge."

They passed through the tunnels on Yerba Buena Island to continue on the second half of the bay bridge.

"So is this your Golden Gate now?" Sten asked.

"Not even close," Hershel chuckled again.

Sten was silent for some time, staring wide-eyed at the rising hills and tall buildings across the water and the traffic that surrounded them. Leaving the bridge he was suddenly startled by a string of Bay Area Rapid Transit cars speeding by on fenced in right-of-way tracks.

"What the hell was that?" he exclaimed loudly.

"Something they call a train," Hershel told him matter-of-factly, "It's like a string of horseless carriages all hitched together to take big groups of people places."

They continued across the city, up and down the hilly streets while Sten's head swung side-to-side trying to make sense of all the sights. They passed the Powell Street cable car, but Sten didn't say a word, too mystified to comment. Finally, they rounded onto the waterfront near Fisherman's Wharf and Sten caught site of the huge golden span that crossed the water at the bay's entrance. King Arthur's Merlin sat speechless in his seat, every now and then starting to say something, but nothing coherent would come out.

Hershel guided their small motor up past the Presidio and onto the wide, high span.

When they exited the bridge into Sausalito, Sten took a series of deep breaths. "I'd ask how men could build such a thing," he said softly, "but with all those tall buildings, that train thing, and, and everything else I'm seeing... Well, I've concluded that you must have cast a spell on me and I'm dreaming all this. It's just too impossible to believe."

"Believe it," Hershel told his friend. "It's all real. But it took people hundreds and hundreds of years to do all these things. That's what this future thing is all about."

"So where are we headed to now?" Sten asked in a voice full of skepticism, viewing the more rural countryside of Marin County.

"You like wine?" Hershel shot back at him.

"Well, yes," Sten replied. "Not as much as ale, but wine is okay, I mean *good* wine."

"My friend Ralph who you met yesterday at the brewery? His parents make some of the best wine you'll ever drink. I thought we might drive up to this place where they give free tastes of their wine, but let me know if you've seen enough of this place, 'cause I'm sure going back to where you want to find this grail thing will be just as weird, compared to our own time, as the things you're seeing here." Sten only nodded his head up and down rapidly.

They arrived at the Edwards Cellars Tasting Room in Napa right about lunch time. It was a few degrees cooler in the wine country. Hershel reasoned that Sten might be best not to sample a bunch of wine on an empty stomach, so he pulled into the drive thru of the local Burger King. At the window, he ordered them each a whopper and more French fries, which they ate in the car at a local park overlooking the Napa River.

"The burger thingies at the brewery were much tastier," Sten told him. "But I still enjoy these, what did you call them? Sandwiches?"

"Well, get your taste buds ready then," King Irv's Merlin told his friend. "This local wine will knock your socks off."

"Socks?" the other man gave him a strange look. "What are socks?"

In ancient England, they covered their feet with what they called hosiery, same principal, but a different animal altogether, really.

"Some kind of future expression I would guess," Hershel said, although Rutherford, back in Oxford had actually given him a pair of socks from Marks and Spencer's at one time, explaining that he could use them to keep his feet warm indoors when he didn't feel like wearing boots. But that was too much to explain to a confused 'old Englander' right now. "Suffice it to say, you will really like this wine."

FIFTEEN

Sten *did* like the California Cabernet wine from the Edwards Cellars, probably a little too much. After the free samples, he begged Hershel to buy them a bottle, and then another. Knowing his own limitations, Hershel sipped slowly while Sten appeared to guzzle. When the Merlin from the past in the red hula girl shirt started to become an embarrassment, Hershel offered a credit card to pay the tab and poured his protesting buddy into the Fiat where, within a few miles of Napa, the man began snoring loudly.

They drove back down Interstate 80 through light Tuesday night traffic, the volume of which increased with every mile they drove closer to their Berkeley motel. Pulling into the Motel 8 lot, Hershel attempted to extract the dead weight of his fellow man of magic from the small car with little luck. He ended up slapping the man into semi-consciousness to get him on his feet. He then walked the drunken time traveler up the back stairs to their room, one arm around his shoulder and the other behind his back, firmly gripping the waistband of the drunk's blue jeans to hold him upright.

Hershel dumped Sten into the room's bathtub. He considered running cold water from the shower over the man, but decided he'd be better to just leave him there to sleep it off. With that dilemma solved, Hershel took some time to study the courtesy maps of the Bay Area the hotel left for guests. When he had seen what he wanted, he tucked himself under the crisp clean sheets of one of the room's double beds and was quickly in dreamland.

Meanwhile, back in the Wholesale Kingdom, King Arthur paced incessantly back and forth across King Irv's parlor. "Where could they be?" he kept asking, his face a mask of concern.

"There's a lot to see in this future California place," King Irv told him for maybe the fiftieth time, taking another drink from his flagon of ale and stroking the ginger cat in his lap. "They'll be back when they've seen enough. What good does worrying do you, anyway?"

"Easy for you to say," King Arthur squealed. "You and I, we're men of the world. We go out each day to face adversity. We fight all manner of man, beast and dragon, always ready for the unknown or the unexpected.

"But poor Sten? He's a scientist, a poor sheltered academic. What could he know of the world's traps and pitfalls? He's like an innocent child, I think of him as, well, as *my* child in a sense."

"Hey, Arthur, stop worrying." Irv told him, again like so many times before. "My Hershel is a man of science too, but he knows how to handle himself. And he's had lots of experience traveling around this future world. I'm sure they're both perfectly safe and having the time of their lives."

"If you say so, Irv," Arthur bleated in a voice full of skepticism. "Maybe I should have another pint of ale to try and calm my nerves."

"Wendy," King Irv called to his serving wench, "Draw another pint of ale for my most special guest, would you please?"

The girl delivered Arthur his drink and the good king took a deep draught, then started in again. "You say your Merlin knows his way around this place he's taken Sten?"

Irv turned his attention to the large ginger tabby cat in his lap and tried to ignore his guest. He stroked Bird's soft tummy-fur while Arthur mumbled more of his misgivings about letting his man travel through time. Then, in a louder voice he finally announced, "I'm anxious and feeling a bit weary." With that, King Arthur drained his ale mug and headed up the stairs to the guest suites.

"See you in the morning," Irv called after him. "Maybe we can get in a round of golf."

SIXTEEN

Wednesday morning, the California mercury seemed to be rising even faster. After another free motel breakfast bar, Hershel decided to take Sten to the beach. While Arthur's Merlin had been snoring in the bath tub the previous evening, Hershel had studied the city map he found on the motel's bureau and plotted a course for their next adventure. He tried to think of a place where they wouldn't encounter too much alcohol. If Sten behaved, they'd end their day back at Ralph's Metaphysical Brewing Company for a pint or two before heading back to their own time and the Wholesale Kingdom.

Once more, they crossed the Oakland Bay Bridge, but today, when they exited the freeway, Hershel found the thoroughfare called Fulton Street from his study of the map and headed due west. Sten was mesmerized as they came along beside Golden Gate Park.

"A lovely forest to one side of us and so much noise and city on the other," he proclaimed. "This future is truly amazing." He then returned to swiveling his head back and forth to take in all his surroundings.

About halfway along, Hershel cut through the park to Lincoln Way, then turned left when it ended at the Great Highway. His passenger stared out the side window at the crashing breakers of the blue Pacific. When they came to Ocean Beach, Hershel parked the Fiat and they got out.

The two men of magic strolled the boardwalk. Sten couldn't help but notice the college and high school girls who had come to the shore on their spring break holiday. He also couldn't believe that people would walk out in public with such scant clothing. He began ogling the young girls so blatantly that Hershel was truly embarrassed.

"Sten," he told his friend, "Can't you keep your eyes in your head? You're drawing too much attention to us. Hey, look at those guys out their surfing. Why don't we watch the surfers?"

"Surfing? Surfers?" Sten mumbled, still following a well-endowed redhead in a thong bikini with his full attention.

"Yeah, out there in the water," Hershel prompted, grabbing his colleague by the shoulders and turning him toward the water. "The guys standing up on those boards out in the waves, they're surfing." He pointed towards three young long-haired boys who'd just caught the curl of a large wave. "Those are surfers. You live on the coast, don't you? Maybe you could take up this surfing and teach some of Arthur's knights how to do it?"

All at once, the beach bunnies were forgotten. In a sort of daze, Sten turned and began slowly stumbling across the hot sand toward the shoreline. "Yes," he mumbled, "Yes that looks like super good fun. How do they do that? How can they stand on the end of such a narrow plank while it flies through the water?"

The pair sat in the shoreline for an hour or so, Sten staring mesmerized out at the young men riding waves and Hershel, totally baked and totally bored, moving his hands around in the warm white sand until he noticed, down the beach, a pair of men with a stack of boards and a sign that advertised surfing lessons.

Hershel had to speak loudly to get Sten's attention. "Sten, hey Sten," he called. "You want to learn to do that? There's someone down the beach offering lessons."

The teacher rented Sten a short board and a pair of swimming trunks. He also had a beach umbrella that Hershel could use to create some shade for himself. The man accepted Hershel's Visa Card to pay for the rental of board, swim suit and umbrella along with a one hour lesson, then pointed out a bath and shower room back by the boardwalk where Sten the Merlin could change out of his clothes.

By the time Sten and his instructor dragged their boards back up onto the sand, Arthur's Merlin had gotten the hang of surfing and had actually caught a couple decent rides on smaller shore-break type waves. The man of magic was also as pink as a boiled lobster, his fair skin fried by the California sunshine.

In spite of his sunburn, Sten's wide grin was almost too big for their small car driving back to Berkeley. He whistled an off-key tune as they drove, every now and then commenting again how much he loved this future land with its nearly naked women and surfing. "I must figure out how to create a surfboard when I returned to the Cornish coast," he told Hershel.

"This future is just the most amazing place," he repeated over and over as they drove across the bay bridge.

It was dark outside by the time they reached Ralph's Metaphysical Brewing Company. The two Merlin's celebrated their day with more Knob Hill burgers and four pints each of Berkeley Bitter ale, then said goodbye to Ralph and staggered out to their Infiniti SUV that would take them back through time to old England.

SEVENTEEN

King Arthur hadn't slept well. He'd tossed and turned, sure that his magician friend was lost somewhere in time never to return. The two English kings were breakfasting on the Warehouse Castle's wide bailey the next morning when Hershel's time machine came shimmering into view just across the golf course. Arthur threw down his fork and serviette at the sight of the contraption's arrival, scrambled to his feet and raced across the wide strip of grass for the Merlin's cave.

Sten, well buzzed on the strong ale he had consumed only moments before although years into the future, stumbled out of Hershel's vehicle, staggered a few steps and threw his arms around his king in a big drunken hug. "Arthur," he slurred, "you would never in a mill'on years believe the things I've seen, ladies walking around on a beach in their undergarments and men riding planks on the ocean. Wha' a fantastic place this future is."

Arthur shook off his Merlin's embrace and angrily turned to King Irv. "Does time travel leave those who try it halfwits? Or does this condition wear off?"

"Relax," Hershel purred, "Sten's just a bit squiffy. We had a few pints just before we left San Francisco and I don't think he's used to the strong ale they brew there."

"Right," Sten barked. "Four pints a' Berkeley Bitter and a big ham'urger."

"A ham'urger?" Arthur questioned, "Is that also a strong drink?"

"He means 'hamburger," King Irv chuckled. "It's something these future folks eat that they call a sandwich, a cut of beef between two pieces of bread. It's quite good, actually." Then, eyeing Sten, Irv commented, "My, you seem to have gotten quite a bad sunburn."

Hershel and Sten, still dressed in their funny Hawaiian shirts and jeans, followed the kings back to their table on the bailey and sat while the monarchs finished their breakfast. Out of the corner of his eye, Hershel saw Wendy approaching with two fresh ales. He turned, shook his head violently side to side and waved her away by thrusting the backs of his hands in her direction. The last thing Sten needed right now was more ale. The poor girl gave a bewildered look, but took the drinks back inside with her.

While the kings dined, Sten told them all about his experiences in a drink soddened voice; the brewery, the bridges, the wine tasting room and the beach. After commenting that his skin felt like he was standing too close to a fire, he went on and on about the beach, drawing confused looks from both kings. Hershel just slowly shook his head while his friend went rattling on.

Their breakfast long since finished, Arthur was showing signs of fatigue at his man's unending chatter. When he could finally get a word in, he suggested that Sten might be tired from his travels. "Maybe you'd like to lay down for a short nap, my old friend."

"And before you do," Irv put in, "I think I should have one of the servants rub some salve on that burnt skin of yours."

Sten could be heard retelling his adventure yet again as he followed his king into the castle and up the stairs to the guest suite.

After the other Merlin was safely off to dreamland, Hershel joined the two kings and Friar Giovanni Agnello, the priest from Vaude Cathedral, in a round of golf. When they returned to the castle from their game, Sten was apparently still fast asleep. The foursome reclaimed their table on the bailey for after game libations, the good friar drinking wine, the others local ale, and discussed how King Arthur's game was coming along.

"I think you're doing remarkably well for someone who's only just learned the game," the friar told Arthur. "God must be looking over your shoulder."

Arthur drew back a bit at the comment, not sure how to take it, but said only, "Thank you."

The quartet was on their second round when Sten came stumbling outside, rapidly blinking his eyes against the bright afternoon sunlight and scratching at his peeling arms and shoulders.

"Welcome back, time traveler," King Irv laughed. "How are you feeling?"

"I think I could use a little hair of the dog," the Merlin said softly, pressing his right palm against the side of his head. After that, he remained remarkably quiet while waiting for Wendy to bring him a flagon of ale. Hershel sighed in relief that Friar Agnello would be spared Sten's long travelogue description.

EIGHTEEN

O ver supper that night, King Irv further questioned Arthur and Sten about this grail object they were seeking. "Do you know just where you're supposed to look? And will you recognize this thing when you see it?"

"Well," Arthur told him. "All these Christians say it's the vessel their savior, Jesus, drank wine out of at the last supper."

"And what does this 'last supper' mean?" Irv further questioned.

"Well, as I understand it," Sten put in, "Some guys took this Jesus out and hung him from a tree or a cross or something, like, they murdered him. I would guess it was the last meal he ate before he was killed."

"That's not much help," Hershel chuckled. "It sounds like we're going on some kind of treasure hunt, but we ain't sure about the treasure. So where was this guy dining, do we know that? Before we can go back in time to look for anything, we have to know exactly where and when."

"Why, in the Holy Land," Arthur told them straight faced. "Probably in the early years of their Christian calendars."

"And where is this Holy Land?" Hershel pushed. "Do you have some idea? I mean, if I'm gonna look for some coordinates on my globe, I'll need to know just where to search."

"Could it possibly be somewhere in Israel?" Irv asked. "That's what our Hebrew people think of as the Holy Land."

"I guess that would be a good place to start," Sten offered with a perplexed look.

"Okay, so it's a Christian thing," Hershel pondered. "Friar Agnello would probably be able to help. He's real knowledgeable about all these ideas. How about tomorrow we go to the cathedral in Vaude and seek an audience with Giovanni Agnello. But I'm not sure how chuffed he's gonna be that we're looking to steal some sacred artifact that belongs to his church people."

The next morning, King Arthur and Sten traveled to Vaude with Hershel and entered the cathedral, where they found Friar Agnello in his office napping with his chin resting peacefully on his chest and a half-finished glass of wine before him.

Hershel softly cleared his throat. When the friar opened his eyes, Hershel asked, "Got a minute, Giovanni?"

"For you and your friends, Hershel? Of course. Would you care for a glass of wine? It's not as good as your cabernet stuff..."

"Wine would be great," Hershel told him nervously.

"Sit down, sit down," the friar beamed. "It's always nice to have company. Not too many people seek me out unless they are troubled. It's good to chat with friends."

Giovanni Agnello uncorked a large jug and filled clay cups for all. When that was done he set the jug on his desk, leaned back in his chair and asked, "To what do I owe the honor of your company today?"

There was some hesitation and further throat clearing around the table until Arthur finally ventured, "Well, we have some questions about your, ah, your faith, I guess."

"Marvelous," the Christian friar beamed again. "I'm always happy to talk about our Lord. It's a topic that never ceases to gladden my heart. Is there a particular scripture in which you're interested?"

"Ur, well, I don't know much about scriptures... it's, uh..." Arthur began.

"It would be this last supper business," Hershel finished for him. "We were wondering about this last supper."

"That would be the dinner our Lord took with his disciples, before he was crucified," Friar Agnello told them with a stern continence.

"And where was that held exactly?" Sten questioned.

"Why, it was in Jerusalem, in the land of Israel."

"One point for King Irv," Hershel mumbled.

"What was that?" Agnello asked.

"Ah, nothing, Giovanni," Hershel replied, casting his eyes downward. "We were just curious about where this ah, crucifixion did you call it? Where this all took place, like, if I were to want to travel there in my time machine."

"Why, you'd be looking for Mount Calvary in Jerusalem," the good friar told them. "And you'd need to go back four hundred ninety two years approximately. We celebrate our savior's crucifixion and resurrection in April, so you'd need to visit there in April, this very month, within a few weeks, actually. Why are you interested in the last supper? Are you thinking of converting to Christianity?"

"Well, not that exactly," Hershel said softly, dragging his right foot back and forth in front of his chair. "I was just thinking that if somebody *should* want to go back there to that time and event, is all."

"It is a special time to us of the faith," Friar Agnello told him, "but I don't think you'd find it a very pleasant place to visit. Those were harsh times compared to the lives we live now."

"Yeah," Hershel drawled, "We were just curious."

"Hershel," the friar said sternly. "I don't think you're telling me the whole story here. What is this really about?"

"Well," Arthur put in, "It's just that King Irv and his people are Jewish, and my people are all Pagans. Sometimes we have a hard time understanding these things."

Giovanni Agnello gave them a questioning look. "And it would help you to understand if you traveled back there in time? Would that make you more inclined to join our faith?"

Arthur let out a nervous laugh. "No, nothing like that. Sorry, forget that we asked."

Friar Agnello's suspicious face turned to a smile. "Would you like some more wine," he asked.

To himself, he thought, something strange is afoot here. I'll get Hershel alone over a few drinks and I'll get to the bottom of this.

NINETEEN

That afternoon found Arthur, Sten and Hershel back in the Merlin's cave intensely studying the globe Rutherford had given Hershel. King Irv's Merlin was frustrated while Arthur and Sten were simply perplexed.

"I can see Israel on this thing," Arthur fumed, "but how do we find Calvary Hill or even Jerusalem, for that matter?"

"If you don't *see* them on there," Hershel told his friends, "There's nothing I can do to make them magically appear."

"Well, how did you find future England in the first place?" questioned Sten.

"Ah, you might say it just found me," Irv's man of magic gave them with a shrug of his narrow shoulders. "I was trying my theory out, I turned the dial, and there I was."

"And this San Francisco place then," Arthur pressed. "How in the devil did you end up there? Sten tells me you know your way around this future California quite well."

"That was an easy one," Hershel smiled. "I had maps of California, lots of really good maps."

"And where did you get these maps?" Arthur inquired. "Surely you can go to the same place and just request maps for this Jerusalem place."

Hershel took a big slug of ale in his frustration, wiped his lips on the sleeve of his robe and shook his head. "King Irv's son-in-law in future England got me maps from someplace called the Royal Automobile Club. They've got lots of maps of that time in the future because people in the future drive their cars, horseless carriages, all over the place on modern roads. But nobody in the future is going driving back into the past, at least not as far back as we're talking about. Why would anyone want maps from so far back in time?"

"Somebody *must* have a use for maps from that time," Arthur argued. "I'm sure there are people interested in ancient history. Let's think about this for a minute. Who would have such an interest?"

"Somebody teaching about history?" Sten replied with a quizzical look.

"Exactly!" Arthur exclaimed. "And who would such a teacher be?"

Hershel took another deep draught of his ale. "Maybe Rabbi Weiss, our teacher, would have such knowledge, but I've been studying in our temple all my life and I've never seen any such maps. There's only the stuff we read in the Torah scrolls... the Christian church maybe?"

"So, I guess we need to go back and see this Friar Agnello chap again," Arthur exclaimed.

Hershel rolled his eyes. "I don't know if that's such a good idea. The good friar looked a bit suspicious the last time we talked to him."

"So are there any *other* Christian fellows you know around here?" Sten asked.

Hershel thought for a minute, then an idea came to him. "There's the Manischewitz brothers, Ernest and Julio. They're the guys who make our wine here in the Wholesale Kingdom. They're Jewish, but they've studied with the Christian monks."

"Wine makers are going to know about places in history?" Sten asked with a confused look. "Why would wine makers know or care about ancient history?"

"No, no," Hershel persisted, "these kids studied winemaking at a Christian monastery a few miles south of our kingdom, a place called Woburn Abbey. It's, like, a big school where Christian monks teach all kinds of things, maybe even ancient geography. And if they teach such a thing, they'll have maps."

"And you think these monks will just surrender these maps to us?"

"Uh, no, your highness, I'm sure they would not. What we'll have to do is take Ernie and Julio into our confidence, let them know what we're trying to find, and then bribe them to get the maps for us from the monks they know at the abbey."

"This is getting very complicated," Sten sighed. "I thought it would just be a simple matter of getting into your time contraption, going back and grabbing this grail thing and Bob's your uncle. I guess nothing's ever as easy as it sounds."

Hershel poured them each another tankard of ale and the trio sat deep in thought for some time. "I can invite the Manischewitz brothers over for a drink," he told his cohorts. "I think they'll be willing to help. They kinda owe me one because I got them the Cabernet grapes to make their special wine, but that's a long story."

"Could we have King Irv talk to them?" Arthur asked, to which Hershel exploded, "No! My God no. We don't want Irv to know that we're asking them to help. I don't think he'd approve at all. Don't mention the brothers or the abbey to King Irv."

TWENTY

Ernesto and Julio were more than happy to take a few hours out from their wine making to meet with Hershel and his guests. They set up a rendezvous for the next afternoon at Debbie's Roadside Attraction Wine Bar and Pizza Café. Debbie was the twin's older sister and had helped to finance their wine making studies with the good monks at Woburn Abbey some years before.

Debbie saved Arthur and Hershel's party a table in the rear of the cafe, far away from the pen of Smokey, the attraction's tame dragon who served to draw curious crowds to the pizzeria. She left two bottles of wine on the table for King Arthur's group, along with a large cheese and fish pizza that they could munch on while they talked.

On his way to the meeting, King Arthur stopped in the large field of stones behind the attraction to check on the encampment of his knights and vassals. He found his men both well and happy. His knights had discovered the pizzeria early on and had developed a fondness for both the establishment's cheap red Dragon's Blood wine and this interesting new pizza dish. They were also fascinated by Smokey, the tame dragon that would dance for them while they drank their wine. No one seemed to be homesick for Cornwall or in any way unhappy with their current assignment to this, to them, distant land.

The Manischewitz brothers had, of course, heard all the New Testament stories in their time studying at Woburn Abbey, so they were familiar with the tale of the last supper and the Holy Grail, but hadn't given any of this Christian stuff a thought since their graduation from wine making school at the abbey.

"Sure, they have classes about geography there," Julio assured King Arthur. "It's part of what they refer to as 'Bible Study,' but I've never seen any maps of these Bible places. They just talk on and on about places like the Sea of Galilee, Bethlehem and the River Jordan. But I'm sure they must have some kind of maps if you pressed them about it."

"But that's just it," Sten told the twins. "We don't want to press them about anything. We want to be as secretive as possible. We want to find out about where these places are, but we don't want anyone wondering why we might want to find such things."

"Maybe if you go down there and sign up for one of their classes?" Ernesto offered.

"Sten, you always like learning new things," Arthur grinned.

"In a Christian monk's school?" Sten howled.

"Remember why we're doing this," Arthur reminded him. "If we can get our hands on this grail thing..."

"Will these monks have me hung as a spy if they catch me?" Sten asked Hershel in a fearful voice.

King Irv's Merlin laughed at the thought. "At the worst, they'll probably hug you and try and convert you to their beliefs. These monks are peaceful guys; at least that's what Giovanni tells me. If they get really mad at you, they'll probably just throw you out and banish you from returning. Something they call excommunicating you from their church."

Sten gave Arthur beseeching eyes that said, "Must I do this?" Arthur's own eyes answered, as did his voice. "I hope you'll enjoy your studies at Woburn Abbey, my friend."

"Hey, they're very free with the wine down there," Hershel added with a big grin.

Debbie came to join them when the rush of tourists had slowed. Hershel made introductions around the table and Debbie was impressed to be meeting a king from so far away across their small island.

"So what brings you to our Wholesale Kingdom?" she asked King Arthur.

"You might say we have some business with your good Merlin, Hershel," he told her with a guarded face.

"Like, something to do with his time travel thing," she laughed. "I knew the word would get out and people would be curious," she winked at Hershel but he returned only an uncomfortable gaze.

"So, what do you think of our pizza?" she asked, changing the subject. "If it wasn't for Hershel's time travel thingy, we'd never have discovered this tasty dish."

Arthur and Sten both nodded their approval.

"Princess Judith, King Irv's daughter, showed me how to make it," Debbie told them. "She was my best friend. She lives in the future now, but she's still here in my heart." The girl patted a hand on her chest. "Maybe someday I can go to the future to see her again."

"We're more interested in going back into the past," King Arthur mumbled. When Debbie turned to stare at him, he merely smiled a big smile, as though he hadn't said a word.

"So, what's so interesting in the past?" she prodded. Hershel shook his head, 'no,' but Debbie didn't seem to notice. "All that stuff is been and done," she laughed. "I'm glad to be living here and now, where we have so much to be thankful for."

Arthur sat stone-faced, not knowing if he should say any more to this commoner. Sten was almost on the point of confiding, but seeing his king's attitude, he held his breath.

"Our friends here aren't Jewish," Hershel told her, "but they're not Christians either. Their people were here before the Romans came and have different beliefs from either the Romans or us. They're looking for a link in the history of this island so they can protect their old ways and their faith. It's kinda complicated."

Debbie knitted her brows for a moment, then smiled. "I think I get it. Yeah, I hope you can help then, Hersh. Everyone should be able to connect with their innermost feelings."

☙ TWENTY-ONE ☙

Sten set off the next day, accompanied by Ernesto and Julio, for the abbey at Woburn. He'd resigned himself to do what he had to for his king, although he was not happy with the idea. On the ride down, the twins told him tales of their encounters with the various Roman monks and their local converts who tried endlessly to bring their thinking around to the superstitions of the Christian life.

"We had to be very focused on our winemaking," Julio told the Arthurian Merlin. "These chaps were most persistent, constantly harping on how this savior of theirs could give us eternal life."

"But the way they put away the wine," Ernesto added, "They didn't seem to be very convinced by their own words. I don't believe everything our Rabbi tells us, but at least he seems to be very sure of all the stuff he says." Both twins dipped their heads in an affirmative gesture to punctuate their words.

After hours of riding, the trio found themselves at the monastery gate just east of the King's Highway. A brother in a rough brown robe recognized Julio and Ernesto and rushed forward to welcome them. "The abbot will be so pleased to see you," he shouted, putting his hands together as if in prayer. "We've prayed that you would return and accept our simple life and faith."

Sten cringed at the thought. Just how far would he have to compromise himself to obtain a map of this so-called Holy Land where he wanted to go? Wasn't there any other way? He smiled at the robed monk as the Manischewitz brothers introduced him. "Pleased indeed," he told the man who gave him a low bow and invited him into the monastery grounds.

The brothers led Sten into a tiny office across a small meadow where one of the monks served them each a generous mug of red wine. They waited a tense half hour before the abbot entered. Sten was quite bothered by a bit of art on the wall behind the desk. It was a sculpture of a man in obvious agony suspended from a cross with blood dripping from a wound in his side. Sten shivered visibly each time he glanced up at it. Who would want to celebrate such a painful bit of torture? Is this the fate he might suffer if they discovered that he was only here to steal information from some old maps of their past?

But the abbot who took a seat across from them seemed to be a friendly and compassionate man. He welcomed the Manischewitz brothers warmly, asking about their sister, Debbie, and the health of their good King Irv.

"And who is your friend that comes to call on our humble parsonage?" the man asked after the formalities were addressed.

"Ah, this is our friend, Sten," Ernesto piped up. "He's from a far off kingdom across our land to the west. Sten's really interested in geography and maps and things."

"And history too," Julio put in. "But in his kingdom, they don't have a lot of places of learning. He was telling us he'd really like to discover more, but there was no one that could teach him in, ah, Cornwall was it?"

"Ah, yeah, Cornwall," Sten mumbled, looking down at his boots.

"Splendid," roared the abbot. "We're just beginning a class in the Old Testament next week. We've always got room for one more serious student. Will you be ready to move into our dormitory right away, Sten?"

"Well, I hadn't..."

"He's ready right now," Julio grinned. "Just let us know what the cost of the course and room and board is and we'll have coin of the realm to you before the study begins, as a donation, I mean."

Sten turned his head to scowl at each of the twins in turn, then focused a wide, false smile on the abbot before him.

"I'll have Brother Raymond show you to your cell," the abbot told Sten as he rose from his seat to depart.

"Thanks a lot, guys," Sten aimed at Ernesto and Julio.

"Isn't this what you wanted?" Ernesto asked with a blank look.

"What *King Arthur* wants," Sten demurred. "I'd rather forget this whole thing right now."

"Hey, it won't be that bad," Julio winked at him.

"We survived their wine making course and lived to tell about it," his twin commented. "See you in a month or so."

"And in the meantime, Hershel can be cleaning up his time thingy and getting it all ready to go back to the past."

TWENTY-TWO

King Arthur was not happy about the delay they would have to endure while Sten attended classes at Woburn Abbey. "There must be an easier way to find the place we're seeking in the past," he fumed over diner with King Irv and Queen Sophie. "Your Merlin has this secret to travel across time. Why can't he just visualize where he wants to be and, and *go* there?"

"As I understand it," King Irv replied patiently, "it just isn't all that simple. If time travel was easy, everyone would be doing it."

"Believe you me," Queen Sophie put in. "I've been to this future place a few times. Ain't nothin' simple about it."

"You're a braver soul than I," Lady Guinevere smiled. "I don't even like traveling across country, all this camping out and riding horses the whole day long. If it was up to me, I'd stay home in my nice secure castle at Tintagel with a few of my good king's knights to look after me."

Arthur shot her a skeptical look, then aimed an evil eye at his man, Sir Lancelot. "I think I can understand what you're getting at," he shot at his lady, then he turned a smile towards his host and commented, "This beef is excellent, King Irv. My compliments to your good chef."

Sir Lancelot blushed deeply, avoiding the eye of his king, but nothing more was said. Lady Guinevere focused on her Cabernet wine and looked away from her husband. Irv and Sophie could both feel the tension, but what could they say?

"It's good to have you here," King Irv told his guest. "We can get in a few good days of golf while we wait for Sten to return. I've got my son, Sol, on tap for tomorrow with Rabbi Weiss to round out our foursome. We should have a great game."

King Arthur kept his eyes down toward his plate of food and didn't answer. This was all, truly, much more than he had bargained for. He only hoped that, in the end, possessing this Holy Grail thing would be worth all he was enduring here.

"More wine, or maybe some ale, Arthur?" Queen Sophie asked.

"Yes, some ale would be nice," Arthur mumbled. "I very much appreciate your hospitality, kind lady."

When Wendy arrived with a frothing mug of ale, Arthur took a long drink, set the vessel down and dabbed at his lips with his serviette, and then his face brightened somewhat.

"I have an idea," he said, looking directly at King Irv. "This golf game is good fun and all, but while we're waiting for Sten to return, why don't my knights engage in a few days of sport with your good men. We could have a jolly tournament of skills, you know, jousting, swordsmanship, horse racing. It looks like you've plenty of room to host such an event up there by your field of stones. Golf is good for us noblemen, but such a tournament could include everyone and make us all participants."

"That sounds like super fun," Sophie nodded. "We can invite good King Richard's knights from Vaude as well, couldn't we Irv?"

"Wendy, could I have an ale as well?" King Irv asked, then he turned back to his guests. "This could take a bit of organizing," he told them. "I'd like to put my son, Prince Sol, and his friend

King Richard, in charge of setting this up. And I would also like to give my men a week or so to practice and hone their skills a bit. We don't see much action around our area, so while I believe my troops are in an acceptable level of readiness, I'd like them to work on these fighting skills before they face such a formidable group as your own well traveled and experienced fellows."

"You give my knights too much credit, sir," Arthur smiled. "But, all the same, my men have been working on their battle arts since we've been here as there isn't that much else to do at our encampment. I'd much rather have them practicing their battle skills then laying about or keeping your local public house open 'til all hours."

"Debbie tells me they have been tucking away some wine and pizza up there at the Roadside Attraction," Queen Sophie giggled.

"Then this tournament will be just the thing for them to work off the extra fat they might be putting on," Arthur smiled back.

Queen Guinevere cast moony eyes across the table at Sir Lancelot. "Lance is the greatest at all these skills," she said dreamily. "Wait until you see him in action," which brought the cross look back to Arthur's face.

No one spoke as they finished their meal. Arthur had two more mugs of ale before Wendy brought the raspberry trifle for their dessert.

When the dinner party finished, Arthur told Sir Lancelot, "I think you had better go up to our encampment and supervise the troops. There's no need for you to hang about our good host's castle until all hours. Lady Guinevere's face registered disappointment, but she took her king's arm with a smile and walked with him up the steps to their lodgings with a sly wink over her shoulder at her husband's principle knight.

TWENTY-THREE

King Arthur's golf game was way off the mark the next day. It was almost as though he'd never had a single lesson or played the game before. He hooked his drives into the rough at almost every hole and spent more strokes retrieving his ball from the few sand traps along the royal course then he did putting on the castle's well tended greens.

The other members of the foursome smiled and reassured him often, but his game just didn't improve. Finally, on the eleventh tee, Arthur confided in his golfing partners. "Damn it, man, I just can't keep my mind on this game when I know my good lady Guinevere is probably entertaining Lancelot somewhere at this very moment. Did I tell you that Lance has leanings toward these Christian beliefs? I'm convinced that he only wants to seduce my queen in order to bring her to this abominable Christian faith."

"How awful," Prince Sol ejaculated. "My own wife, Princess Amy, lies in the spell of these Christians. She spends all her days at the cathedral in Vaude praying and lighting candles. I can't remember the last time she had any desire to…"

"Oh Guinevere has plenty of desire," Arthur barked, "For *Lance*, anyway. Not much more for me it would seem. All these stories about their so-called savior."

"Gentlemen," King Irv interrupted. "We're playing a serious game here. Let's save the gossip and complaining for later over an ale or two. Arthur, you'd be wise to forget these domestic issues for the remainder of the game. It really isn't doing your handicap any good."

"Oh, I suppose you're right," Arthur agreed. "But how would you feel if your good wife..."

"My good wife would *not*." Irv told him with strong conviction. "It would be a sin under our ten commandments and my good lady is a faithful follower of our Torah. Also, Sophie loves me and knows she'd never find a man as kind and understanding as I am." He gave a confident smile to his fellow monarch.

"It must be nice," is all Arthur could manage to mumble in reply.

"So, can we get on with the game already?" Prince Sol asked.

King Arthur's game improved as he put his domestic problems aside for the moment, but in the back of his mind, his anger was smoldering. When they walked from the eighteenth green up to the Warehouse Castle bailey, where Friar Agnello was waiting to join them in a drink, Arthur excused himself to go check his wife's chambers. He returned in time to join his mates for the second round of drinks with a sheepish grin.

"I guess your good Queen Sophie has been entertaining Guinevere for most the day," Arthur announced. "Lancelot has been busy putting my troops through their paces up at our campground."

"And you could have played a much better and more relaxed game," Friar Agnello laughed. "We Christians aren't all that bad," he told the monarch, "although I can't speak for your knight fellow. Are these *Roman* Christians back home in your land that are counseling your knight Lancelot?"

"No, your holiness," Arthur answered politely. "Their friar, Patrick, is an *Irishman*." He spit out the last word as though it had burned his tongue.

"Irishman?" Agnello queried. "What is an Irishman?"

"Ireland is a place across the sea from our Cornish coast. It's a wild, unsettled locale, not at all like our island's many kingdoms. They used to be our allies until this Christian idea took root there. And this Patrick fellow claims to speak for all their people now, speaking out against our Pendragon, our age old traditions and beliefs that we had shared for all time remembered."

"Oh dear," said Rabbi Weiss, placing his left elbow in his right palm and caressing his cheek with his left hand. "This does not portend well."

Arthur raised his clay mug and took a long pull from his ale before slamming the vessel down on the table with a satisfied thud.

"Here, here, my friends," King Irv announced with a smile. "Things are never really as bad as they seem."

"Easy for you to say, Irv" Arthur told him with downcast eyes. "You have a faithful wife and a Christian neighbor that respects your faith and beliefs. I envy you, good sir!"

TWENTY-FOUR

aturday morning rolled around and Sir Shecky, one of King Irv's knights, came into the parlor to interrupt their meeting wearing a strange face. "Your highness," he spoke. "There is a most unusual entourage at our gate."

"Unusual?" Irv asked. "What kind of group would be unusual to our very open and accepting kingdom?"

"Well, highness?" the man gave forth with a clouded face, "they seem to be knights from some far off kingdom, but they also all appear to be, well, ladies."

King Irv proceeded to the portcullis along with King Arthur, surrounded by both knights and servants, to check it out, a female assemblage coming to his doorstep? What could this mean? Had he somehow offended the ladies and mothers of Wholesale Kingdom? And had they somehow brought supporters from other lands to chastise him?

When he arrived at the castle gate, he found standing before him the tallest and thinnest woman he had ever seen, over six feet in height and probably weighing less than eight stone. She had a halo of dark black curls surrounding her thin face and cascading down the back of her suit of armor, and the greenest eyes Irv had ever seen. The good king looked her up and down, unsure of what to say. He finally settled on "Good morning, Madame, how may we be of service to you?"

"I am Anne of Rexia," the woman proclaimed. "I understand that you might be on a maneuver to locate this so called Holy Grail so sought after by the Christian kings."

"Well, the idea has been kicked around by my Merlin, Hershel, and a few other interested parties," Irv laughed.

"One of those parties being Sten, the Merlin of King Arthur?" queried the tall, thin woman as she towered over the Jewish king and tipped her head toward Arthur, the visiting monarch. "Sten implied that I might join him here. I, too, have an interest in this Holy Grail. These Christian kings mock my Druid kingdom because we worship a female God, the God of nature and nurture, as have our sisterhood since the beginning of recorded time."

Sten just happened to be home on leave from classes at the abbey for the week end and hanging out with Hershel, telling him about what he had, and hadn't, learned so far about ancient map making and geography.

King Irv was at a loss for words. He stood aside and motioned the tall fair skinned woman and her league of ladies into Warehouse Castle. As the female group entered the main hall of the castle, Sten stepped forward.

"Anne, baby, so good to see you."

"Don't give me that 'good to see you crap,' Sten," the lanky lady replied with a snarl. "We had a mutual pact to find this Holy Grail thing and then you skipped out on us. So what's going on here?"

"Anne, baby, don't get your panties in a twist," Sten crooned. "I met this other Merlin that has a time machine which can take us back to get the Grail right from the source. I was planning to cut you in just as soon as I found out if it was legit."

"Yeah?" the tall woman replied. "So I'm here now and you can introduce me to your friend with the time machine and we'll all do this thing together."

As they spoke, Hershel entered from the rear of the hall. "And here he is now," Sten beamed. "Hershel, my friend, I want you to meet Anne of Rexia. Anne, this is Hershel, a fellow Merlin. Hershel has perfected travel across time."

"Perfected?" Hershel laughed, looking the tall woman up and down. "I don't know about perfected, but I've been able to get around to a few places. Can we offer you a drink? We have some great Cabernet wine from the future. I know you ladies tend to go for wine."

"Wine?" the tall woman scoffed, "I'll have ale, just like you men drink. And some for my group of ladies as well"

"I'm not exactly the landlord here," Hershel cautioned. "Hey, Irv, can we have some ale for our lady guests?"

King Irv was all smiles. He summoned his servants to bring drinks for Anne and her entourage, then turned to Sten and quietly hissed, "You invited people to my kingdom without a word to me? I find this to be most impertinent. We'll have words with your good king about this."

Arthur stepped back from the group into a dark alcove, his face a mask of humility, as if to say, "I knew nothing of this."

Sten gave a shrug of his shoulders. "Highness," he demurred, "I didn't exactly invite them here... I, well..."

"But they're here now," King Irv told him with a face as close to anger as King Irv's face ever achieved. "And I have to deal with them. Where's King Arthur? I'll want to have words with your king, and soon."

Sten cast his eyes down at the tips of his boots without a reply as Arthur continued to back away into hiding.

Sir Shecky dispatched a rider up to the field of stones, where some of Irv's knights were having friendly games of battle skills with King Arthur's men. Sir Lancelot, upon hearing that Anne of Rexia was at King Irv's door, quickly brought more of their king's knights and they were standing before their host within less than an hour, but Anne had departed.

"I did *not* invite this lady to your kingdom," Arthur swore to Irv when he finally advanced from his hidey-hole. "I try to discourage her from visiting my own court as much as I can, though Sten seems to have some kind of fondness for the woman, I can't understand why. She seems to harbor the idea that women are as fit to rule as men, imagine that!"

King Irv gave a thoughtful smirk. "I'm not sure that sex has anything to do with fitness to rule over people," he ventured. "I know we've always had male kings in the past, but in future England, where my daughter Princess Judith lives, they have a queen as head of state and they seem to be doing quite well."

King Arthur gave a troubled snort. "A queen? On the throne of England? You've got to be joking." Lancelot and the rest of Arthur's knights slapped each other's shoulders and laughed as well.

"Ask Hershel," Irv said with confidence, "he can tell you all about Queen Elizabeth the Second, and her ancestor, the first Queen

Elizabeth many years before her. And between these two, they had Queen Victoria for some sixty-four years."

"You're sure of this?" Arthur shrieked in amazement. "This future must be a strange land indeed." King Irv simply smiled.

"So, now, how do we deal with this Anne woman?" he asked Arthur.

"After what you've just told me," came the reply, "I don't know how to answer. I guess we'd better sit her down at the table and negotiate with her. But if she wants to be cut in on our search for the Holy Grail, she will have to pay her fair share."

TWENTY-FIVE

W endy drew tankards of ale for Anne and her most senior knight, Lady Oprah, when they returned as Irv granted them seats at the table along with himself, Arthur, and Sir Lancelot.

"My Merlin, Hershel, did invent a time machine," Irv confessed. "He often goes to the future, but, to my knowledge, he's never attempted to travel back through the past of our history. Good King Arthur has come here to ask if such a thing is possible, and my Merlin is working long hours with Sten, Arthur's own Merlin, to establish if this can be done."

"And I'm sure it can be done," roared Queen Anne indignantly, drumming delicate fingers on the tabletop.

"Well, that remains to be seen," King Irv continued, unruffled by the lady's rudeness. "I'm sure all things are possible if we can just understand how the world works. Unfortunately, our Rabbi has found nothing in the Torah that could explain such phenomena to us, so we must rely on what Hershel, my good Merlin, reports to me.

"At this very moment, Sten is studying ancient geography to try and establish coordinates where my man, Hershel, can focus his time thingy to locate this so-called Holy Grail."

"But Sten is *here*," Anne scoffed, "drinking ale and having good times with you and your men. Why is he not studying harder to do this thing for us all?"

"Sten is taking geography classes with the Christian brothers at Woburn Abbey," Hershel chuckled, entering the room. "They gave him a few days off for some kind of Christian holy day, Easter or something they called it, so he's back here with us for the week end, but he has to return to the abbey Monday morning." Hershel dragged Sten into the chamber and slapped him on the back playfully, "Poor fellow."

"And what have you learned so far?" Queen Anne pressed. "Do you have any real insight as to where you might find this grail thing?"

"Hey, give me a break," Sten whined. "I've only been in this class for a week. And, so far, all these blokes are talking about is something they call 'salvation,' or some such nonsense. We probably won't be getting to view actual maps for another fortnight."

"We can wait," Lady Oprah told him, folding her arms across her small, pert breasts.

"You can't wait here in my castle," King Irv roared. "King Arthur is already occupying my guest suites."

"I couldn't help but notice that Arthur's men are camped just to the north," Anne told him. "It's a large, open space. My good ladies will set up camp for me there as well. We've been told there's a café by those fields that sells an interesting dish they call pizza. I think it will be a most suitable accommodation for my troops."

Queen Sophie, who'd been lurking in the hallway and overheard much of the conversation, entered the room and clapped her hands together. "Oh grand," she gushed. "Queen Anne's knights can take part in our tournament as well. It will be such a memorable event."

King Irv and the Holy Grail

Both Arthur and Irv shot daggered eyes at Queen Sophie. Lady Knights had no place in games that simulated combat.

Reluctantly, King Irv escorted Anne of Rexia to the field of stones north of his castle and showed them to an area beyond where Arthur's men were camped. "I trust this will be satisfactory to you, my good lady?" Irv queried.

"Don't try to patronize me because I'm a female," Anne bellowed. "We can sleep right up there among the rocks if we have to. We are not, as some say, the weaker sex or the meeker sex, at least not where I come from. We can hold our own against you or any of your men any day. And we'll show you this in your tournament." Then she gave King Irv a dazzling smile. "But, in your heart of hearts, you already know this." And, making her face very serious again, she finished, "Just don't try to fuck with me, your highness!"

TWENTY-SIX

Queen Anne returned to Warehouse Castle the next evening as Irv and Sophie's dinner guest. King Irv sat in his customary place at the head of the table with Anne directly to his right and Queen Sophie to his left. Sten and Hershel joined them, but Arthur had excused himself, wishing to dine with Guinevere and his men at the village pub in Wholesale. The western king wanted to discuss the idea of a tournament with his noble knights and help select who would be best to represent his kingdom in each area of sport. Lady Oprah was at the end of the table, taking notes.

As King Irv and his guests broke bread, Anne asked his Merlin if he would tell her about his travels across time and space. Hershel was only too happy as he loved to talk about himself and his accomplishments. He made a point of avoiding talk of his first trip through time, where his machine had landed on a drug dealer, killing the man, beginning his tale instead with his second trip forward in time and his meeting Rutherford, the black professor, who was now King Irv's son-in-law.

"Oh course, he wasn't a professor yet," Hershel chuckled, "that came later."

Hershel went on to explain how he had discovered canned ale and learned to play golf, and how, when he returned with the dish they call pizza, Irv's daughter, Princess Judith, had quickly figured out how to prepare the dish, using the fiery breath of her tame pet dragon to sufficiently cook the dough and melt the cheese.

"Later on," he bragged, "After Princess Judith went to live in the future and Rutherford got his teaching spot at Oxford University, I got to play golf with all these hot shot professor friends of his."

At this, Anne held up her hand, palm out, to stop Hershel's narrative. "You say you played golf with these learned men from this, what did you call it, university of higher education? Did you get to meet any that taught world history, or possibly Christian history?"

"Well," Hershel hemmed, "Rutherford took me to the Jewish Studies Center in Oxford once."

"That might be a help," Anne replied thoughtfully. "They would certainly *know* about ancient Israel in the time of this Christian man, Jesus. But didn't you tell me earlier that your own Rabbi only has words on scrolls and not maps?"

"Well, yeah," Hershel told her, "So what's that got to do with the price of fish?"

"I think you might find that these friends of King Irv's son-in-law who teach men and women about history will have more than just old scrolls. They should be in possession of very good maps of this old Israel. Possibly even maps that you can buy and bring back here to study and plan where you will need to go to locate this last supper event and the Holy Grail we seek."

Hershel slapped his forehead with the palm of his right hand. "What was I thinking... or not thinking, of course they would. I'll just need to go spend a few days with Rutherford and the Princess."

"Uh, does that mean I don't have to go back to Woburn Abbey," came a hesitant beseechment from Sten. "I'd really rather just stay here with all of you."

Anne thought for a minute in silence, her head tipped slightly to one side. "No, Sten," she finally answered. "I believe we should keep all our bets covered. These monks might have more authentic maps as they are closer to the actual time in history where you want to arrive. You get what you can from the monks and we'll compare it to whatever Hershel might bring back from this future university."

"You are one smart lady," Hershel cried out. "It's a good thing you showed up here when you did."

King Irv grinned. "Good King Arthur may not share your opinion," he told his Merlin.

So on Monday morning, Sten returned to Woburn Abbey and Hershel departed for future England. Anne of Rexia remained in the Wholesale kingdom as a sort of thorn in King Arthur's side. While their troops were camped side-by-side, Queen Anne's ladies made a big show of gearing up for the forth coming tournament. Her female knights jousted and fought in the fields alongside Arthur's knights, displaying some amazing concentration and skill, enough that more than one of King Arthur's fellows came to their king with questions about how they might deal with these female fighters. After all, they had all been brought up to give any female passing respect and then avoid them, unless they had some amorous feelings for the lady.

King Arthur instructed them to show no mercy. "These ladies are rebels and upstarts," he told his men. "We can not let them show us men up. We must do our best to put them in their place. Do you understand what I'm saying?"

Sir Lancelot shot him a bewildered look, but others of Arthur's famous round table nodded agreement. "We will best these upstart females," Sir Reginald assured him, "No matter what the cost."

"Thank you," Arthur told Sir Reginald, laying a hand on the knight's shoulder. "I'm glad you understand what we're dealing with here."

And for the next few weeks, Arthur's good knights practiced hard, perfecting every skill they had previously learned. But they couldn't help but notice that the ladies of Rexia were doing the same and often doing it better, smoother and with more aplomb.

Sir Lancelot feared reporting such things to his king and so just kept pushing his men harder, increasing the hours they spent in training. And all the while, he observed Queen Anne of Rexia watching from the sidelines with a tankard of ale in her hand, laughing at his efforts. What did this woman want of him, he thought to himself?

Meanwhile, Sten remained at Woburn Abbey, bored by the endless lectures about the Christian savior and his many attributes. No one had any maps of this Holy Land to share, at least not at his level of study. He dozed through the endless lectures of Bible study, unable to comprehend what these crazy monks were going on about. They had nothing to say about the old Gods or the sacred Arthurian Pendragon. It was all so confusing and one-sided. So Sten just nodded off through the lectures, hoping he'd wake up when they brought out the maps he was looking for.

TWENTY-SEVEN

Hershel returned after seven or eight days with copies of some old maps that one of Rutherford's professor buddies had given him. These old charts showed Jerusalem circa the year 30 by the Christian calendar, with clear markings for the old marketplace, Calvary Hill and the surrounding countryside. From this, Hershel surmised, they could easily find the Garden of Gethsemane, highlighted on the map, at the foot of the Mount of Olives. And once they landed in this place, they were almost home free to grab this Holy Grail thing.

For comparison, Princess Judith had given Hershel modern Royal Auto Club maps of Israel and of Jerusalem and its surrounding neighborhoods, but the man of magic wasn't quite sure what to make of these. The borders at the edge of these modern maps had bold, red- lettered warnings about terrorist threats and bombs. Was this something new, or did he need to lookout for bad people beyond the bad guys who planned to murder this Jesus character?

Back in his cave, Hershel was able to compare the maps with the surface of his globe, just as he'd done with the San Francisco and California maps for his earlier adventures. The only thing left to establish was the exact moment in time when this last supper thing had occurred. He hoped that Sten's study with the monks of Woburn Abbey could solve this last piece of the puzzle for them.

He could hardly wait to deliver the new information he had to his king. He wasn't that concerned about helping this crazy western king, Arthur, but he somehow knew that knowledge of this Holy Grail thing could guarantee his own monarch a place in history.

Hershel left his laboratory and ventured up to Warehouse Castle only to find that King Irv was somewhere out on the back nine of the royal golf course in a foursome with his son, Prince Sol, Rabbi Weiss and Friar Agnello. He asked Wendy to fetch him a tankard of ale and slouched in a large chair out on the castle bailey with his feet up on a table. Staring out at his cave across the broad expanse of the second fairway, Hershel realized how happy he was to be back in his own time. Modern Oxford had been quite an exciting rush when he'd first discovered this distant, time wise, land, but all the noise and traffic got old quickly. It was always nice to come home where breezes parted the trees, birds sang and life was simple.

When the foursome returned, Irv invited his golfing buddies to have a few drinks with him. "Oh, hello Hershel," he greeted his Merlin. "I see you've started without us. We'll have to get a few pints for ourselves and get caught up. So what do you have to tell us?"

While Hershel was anxious to relay what he'd learned to King Irv, he wasn't sure if it was something he should share with too many others.

"Not a lot, highness," he shrugged nonchalantly. "I'll catch you up later after I've had a chance to compare notes with Sten."

Irv gave a questioning look, but let the subject drop. Instead, they discussed how Friar Agnello had lately developed a tendency to hook his balls into the rough on the longer holes. The Rabbi suggested that Giovanni Agnello might put a bit more bend in his knees when raising his club behind him in preparation for long shots. The others nodded their agreement and signaled Wendy for more ale.

By the time the party broke up, Hershel was about to piss his drawers with excitement about the news he had for his monarch. "Will you be joining us for dinner, Hershel?" Irv asked with a grin.

"Ah, yeah, sure, highness, but I think we should talk first," Hershel gushed forth.

"But it's the dinner hour now, Hershel. The queen will be expecting us at any minute."

"Who else is gonna be at the royal table tonight?" Hershel queried, "King Arthur or any of his crew?"

Irv gave Hershel his most charming smile. "I believe it will be just you, me and the queen. Prince Sol might drop in, but he hasn't indicated that he plans to."

The Merlin breathed an audible sigh of relief. "Great," he exhaled. "I've got some maps and things from Rutherford, but it's kinda like, for your eyes only... That's like, a line I borrowed from some modern movie Judith and Rutherford took me to see about some English superman who protects the queen in the future."

"You must tell me all about it some time, this movie I mean. For now, come and find your seat at my table. We'll be having some very fine roast beef tonight."

TWENTY-EIGHT

The main course was served, followed by some other salady dishes with kale, cucumber and tomatoes. Hershel cleaned his plate and smiled at his king and queen until Sophie excused herself to check on the kitchen staff. As soon as she had left the room, Hershel bounced up, full of life.

"Highness," he cried in a loud whisper, "I got the maps we need. Rutherford gave me enough information that I'm sure I can find this place on my globe and program it into the time machine. I'll let you break the news to King Arthur, and I hope you can extract a good price from him if we can locate this grail thing he wants."

"Hershel," King Irv grinned. "It's not just about making money off this thing. We want to gain some acceptance from these Christians. If we can just get them all to accept us as equals, the way the good kingdom of Vaude does here with us that would be worth more than money could buy. I think that's what Arthur is seeking."

"But we will be asking a price from Arthur if we succeed," Hershel asked with a straight face.

"Of course," King Arthur replied with a wide grin. "We should be doing all this for nothing? I don't think so."

Hershel gave his king a high-five with a big grin. "Cool, your highness. That's why I wanted to speak with you in private."

"Don't worry, Hershel," Irv replied. "If nothing else, I've got a good head for business."

Wendy was there right away with more ale for the two. "Your highness has it all together tonight?" the serving girl asked with a wink and a grin.

"More than you could know." Irv told her, "and thank you for asking."

"I've confided a bit in the staff," King Irv told Hershel, holding his left finger at the side of his nose in a "you ain't seen me" gesture. Hershel just grinned and nodded.

"So what exactly have you told them?" Hershel asked with a concerned look.

"Only that they shouldn't trust whatever Arthur and his men might tell them," Irv chuckled. "I just don't want these Tintagel people corrupting or compromising our own folks."

"Is there a danger in that?" Hershel asked.

"There's *always* a danger," King Irv replied. "These people don't follow our same beliefs, they haven't studied the Torah, and so how are we to trust them?"

"I guess I see your point, highness," Hershel shrugged. "And in these crazy times, is there anyone we can trust?"

"Exactly," Irv grinned. "You'll be taking Sten to this past location, so I'll trust *you* to keep an eye on him and make sure he doesn't screw up anything in the past that will irreversibly change our own time or the future beyond us. You're the only person I can trust with such a responsibility."

Hershel returned to his cave with this heavy burden on his shoulders. Funny, he thought, as a Merlin he had never had to take any responsibility. His life had been the simple day-to-day joy of experimenting with science and presenting new ideas to his monarch. Suddenly he was the only person King Irv could trust? This did not seem like a Merlin's role at all. What had he done to deserve this?

Damn that Sten! And why had he agreed to go to that convention in the big city? He should have known better. But that was past history now. Hershel figured he'd better pull up his socks and do what his king requested. The sooner he had finished with all this Holy Grail business, the sooner he could get back to his simple life of toying with the universe and playing the occasional round of golf.

Hershel returned to his cave and spent the night comparing the maps he'd received in future England with his globe, then calculating how and where he'd have to send his little tin travel machine.

Although history had often changed the political landscape of ancient Israel, much of it after his own time, Hershel was able to come up with some pretty solid coordinates. When the sun peaked over the forest to the east, he sent a messenger up to King Arthur's camp that Sten should join him as soon as possible. They were almost ready to begin their adventure.

TWENTY-NINE

F inally, the morning arrived. Hershel's calculations, checked and double-checked, seemed to indicate an exact location in both time and space for the event the Christians had dubbed The Last Supper.

They awoke at dawn and went down to find King Irv, King Arthur and their ladies seated at the table with a big spread of breakfast including eggs, bacon, baked beans, fried tomatoes, porridge, bagels and lox.

King Arthur was a one-man cheering squad as his and King Irv's Merlins tucked away their food. Irv and Sophie simply smiled their confidence in Hershel beyond question. When the two men of magic got up from the table to head across the golf course for Hershel's time machine, King Irv and Sophie gave them a simple, "Mahzel." King Arthur was much more effusive, cheering on the two men of magic and telling them, over and over, how everything depended on their journey and he had every faith in them.

Hershel walked around his contraption, giving it a last minute safety inspection before taking his seat at the controls; no loose panels, antenna tightly fastened and solar crystals all securely attached. Behind his seat, he had packed a few cans of Ale and a basket of sandwiches, just in case they got stranded somewhere. He then motioned for Sten to get into the craft with him and prepare for liftoff.

Hershel and Sten sat back and closed their eyes briefly. When they opened them, they were in a hot, dry desert place. It had to be at least one-hundred degrees outside. The time machine was like a sauna bath seconds after they landed. Crowds of dark, bearded men in long robes milled about by a large rock of a hill. A winding trail led up the side of the mount to a sort of cathedral looking structure. A fellow in a light blue yarmulke and a white robe with sky-blue trim stepped forward saying, "Welcome to Jerusalem. So where did you come from, already? A minute ago this was an empty space and, whoosh, here you are? And what's that funny tin hut you just stepped out of? Oy, I've seen some bad housing, but *tin*, as hot as this place gets?"

"Don't ask, you wouldn't want to know," Hershel replied to the man with a lopsided grin.

"Some kind of secret Roman spies, are you?" the serious faced man in the yarmulke questioned. "There seem to be quite a few of you around right now."

"No, really" Hershel assured him. "I'm a good Jewish boy just like you, no Roman blood at all, though I've drank a bit of their wine in my time.

"Maybe you could help me. We're looking for the place where they're going to be holding some kind of last supper event."

"Oy, followers of that Jesus fellow, are you. Well, let me tell you, I'm kinda fond of the man. He seems to be good people, with his heart in the right place, but, oy, what a stink he's stirred up here of late. I don't know…"

"That's the guy;" Sten put in. "Is he around here somewhere?"

"Listen, you don't want to find him right now," the stranger told them. "Word is they're gonna crucify him soon."

"Crucify?" Sten queried.

"Like nail him up on a big wooden cross already. Where are you guys from anyway? You don't know crucify? You can't be from around here."

"We're from England, actually," Sten told the man, which brought further confusion.

"Och, so where is this England then?"

Again, Hershel told him, "You don't want to know. So, if they're holding a big dinner for someone like this Jesus fellow, where would be the likely place they'd have it?"

The stranger thought for a minute, scratching his head under his blue head cover, then pulling at his beard. "Not Casa Napoli, that would be all Roman fare, probably full of pork... I would guess it would have to be Mordechai's All Kosher Grill and Bar, down in the heart of the old town. But they don't open until nightfall. You might want to get in out of the heat until then. You'll seriously bake in that tin thing of yours."

Sten and Hershel pushed the time machine into a small, seemingly vacant cave at the base of the rock and took off on foot through the old city. They found a wine bar in another small cave nearby and ordered some of the Roman red, then settled in to wait for the sun to go down.

"What a God-forsaken place this is," Sten whispered when the barman had turned away. "One could fry eggs on the ground here. Why would anyone in his right mind want to live here?"

"According to the Rabbi," Hershel told him, "it beats the hell outta living as slaves in Egypt. That's all I know."

"And, so where is this Egypt place?" Sten inquired.

"Across something called the Red Sea," Hershel answered. "I could show you on the map. Didn't you ever study the Torah?"

"What's a Torah?" Sten parroted back.

Hershel gave his friend a look that said the man must be a simpleton.

"Well?" Sten pressed.

"Never mind," Hershel told him, taking a deep drink of his wine. "I guess it ain't a part of your people's history like it is mine. My people were held as slaves in this Egypt place, like forever, and a wise dude named Moses pulled some fast moves to get us away from there. Our Torah scrolls tell how our people wandered around in this stinkin' desert for some forty years until we found this place." He spread his arms around to encompass their surroundings. "This hot and dusty locale was to be our promised land."

"I can see why no one else would want to fight you for it. What a wasteland," Sten told him, shaking his head side-to-side.

"Well, I guess the place has got soul," Hershel fired back before finishing his glass and signaling the bartender for another round.

The two drank wine in silence for awhile, then Hershel held up his hand. "So, I'm thinkin', do we have any idea how we're supposed to get a hold of this Holy Grail thing…? Or even how we'll recognize it when we see it?"

"Well…" Sten mused. "Some of these Christian folks say that their Jesus character drank his wine out of it."

"Okay," Hershel countered. "And how do we recognize this Jesus at the supper?"

"Oh, that should be easy," Sten laughed. "All the paintings of him I've seen in these Christian places, he's very pale and English looking. He should stick out like a sheep in a herd of cows from the dark folks we see all around us here."

"Okay," Hershel began again. "And how do we get close enough to this man if we find him, so that we might grab his 'grail' or wineglass or whatever it is from him?"

They both fell silent again, staring into their own wine goblets.

"Maybe if we dress up like waiters at this café?" Sten offered.

"Yeah, that could be a start," Hershel nodded. "As waiters, we'd have a good excuse to be there. And we shouldn't even have to grab the glass from under this guy's nose. We just pocket the thing while we're clearing the tables." Both men smiled and nodded to themselves at this stroke of genius.

After a few more sips of wine, Hershel asked Sten, "So how do the waiters dress in this place?"

"How should I know," Sten roared back. "I've never been here before." Then he took a few deep breaths and sighed, "Sorry, I didn't mean to shout."

The only other customer in the bar, a Roman soldier by his dress, stared at them, then turned back to his own goblet of dago red.

"Maybe we'd better go find this place and have a look around," Hershel suggested. "We need to know the layout before we go in there, and while we're scoping it out, we can see how the staff dress and maybe even borrow a couple of their outfits before any customers arrive.

THIRTY

"**D**o you mean the Holy *Grill*? the man outside of Mordechai's All Kosher Grill and Bar asked them. We'll be preparing the last supper on our open fire out back of the restaurant. I'm sure that's what you're seeking."

Sten elbowed Hershel's side. "Do you see the size of that fire pit? If it's the Holy *Grill* we need to take with us, can we even fit it into your time machine?"

"No way," Hershel mumbled. "Let's just get the wine glass this Jesus guy is drinking from and hope that satisfies whoever Arthur's trying to pass this off to." The two men of magic nodded and shook hands on this, dismissing the Holy Grill and turning their attention to the eatery's arriving staff. They sat down on a large rock near the entrance where they could keep track of the activities surrounding the place. It was hot as blazes while they manned their outpost. As they observed the comings and goings, they noticed that most of the staff arriving for work were wearing gray robes with light blue trim; similar to the people in the streets, but unique enough that they could be recognized as restaurant staff. Each had his name embroidered on the robe's left breast in Hebrew with sky blue thread.

Soon a man approached wearing a white robe with the same blue trim, but an embroidered badge that identified him as Solomon, the maitre d'hôtel. Solomon made a detour in their direction.

"You look a bit scruffy to be patrons of this establishment," he told them, "so why don't you just be moving along. I've got a special party booked in tonight and I don't need any riff-raff hanging around to beg from or otherwise bother my customers. You two can get something cheap to eat at our poor window out in the back; falafels, kabobs or lamb gyros."

Burning under the man's watchful eye, Sten and Hershel headed down the alley toward the back of the place. They arrived by the rear entrance just in time to see a pair of gray-robed employees being sacked for selling places around the last supper to journalists and other interested Roman parties. They watched as the disfavored pair shed their uniforms and were tossed out into the alleyway. They took notice that the restaurant worker who had performed the dismissal had simply dropped the former waiter's robes in a laundry bin on the establishment's back porch.

As soon as the employee entrance door had closed, Hershel and Sten were up there, digging in the hamper and bringing out the robes that had been shed. Fortunately, the garments were all a sort of unisex design. The first uniform was a perfect fit for Hershel. The other discarded robe was a bit tight on Sten's stout frame, but appeared to fit well after they tore out a stretch of the side seams.

The pair crouched by the door and waited. After a few minutes, one of the kitchen prep guys came out with a bucket of wilted greens that he put in the wet garbage bin. Sten and Hershel waited as he opened the back door and headed back to work. At the last possible second, Sten reached out and prevented the door from closing. The future pair then crawled inside after the man and found a dimly lit corner of the kitchen in which they could crouch inconspicuously. From here, they would have to listen closely for any hint that this Jesus fellow and his party had arrived. And what would they do then? Surely someone had been assigned to service this most important table. Nobody would believe that they were the assigned waiters unless they could knock out the primary guys and hide the bodies somewhere.

"Hey," Hershel offered, "How about I shed this servant's garment and just try to approach the table and talk to the man? If I fail and get tossed out on my ear, you're still here to grab the wine glass. Either way, we've got a great chance of copping the thing and bringing it back with us."

"So how about I shed my robe, which isn't exactly a great fit, and you hang around to grab the wine glass?"

"I thought of it first," Hershel grinned. "We'll do it my way."

Twelve dudes who called themselves the great man's disciples arrived pretty much on time, taking seats at the long stone table in the restaurant's banquet room. They arranged themselves from either side of the long bench, leaving two places at the center for their leader and his lady friend. Hershel wished that he could stand up and pace the floor to work off some of his nervousness. He couldn't imagine how Sten was coping, hiding in his dark corner of the establishment's kitchen.

Jesus strolled in forty-five minutes late, arm and arm with a lady they all greeted as Mary. All the guys around the table called him "Jesus," but he was a dark fellow with a sizable nose and black curly hair, looking nothing like all his pictures around the Christian cathedrals.

"My Jesus has so many friends and fans," Mary gushed at them. "It's really hard to get away. Everyone wants to touch his garment and ask for some kind of blessing already."

Jesus patted her hand. "It's okay, fellahs, I'm here now so let the feasting begin." One of the disciple cats gave a nod to the head waiter that he should pour more wine and start serving the main course.

Hershel approached the man before he could sit down. "Listen, you won't believe this 'cause I can hardly believe it myself," he whispered to the guest of honor.

"And who might you be?" smiled Jesus, looking Hershel up and down quizzically.

"Well, that's the first thing," Hershel told him, just a little louder. "Can we step over toward the door here for a minute? I know it might sound a bit fantastic, but I'm a good Jewish boy from the future, like some five-hundred years from now. See, I've traveled through time and where I come from you're, like, a really big noise with most the population, if you know what I mean, but not among *our* people, our *Jewish* people. There's this whole other group of folks that have made you into some kinda God, not a Jewish messiah at all."

"But that's the last thing I want," Jesus demurred. "I'm just a common man with a message that we all have to live together and love one another."

"I can dig that, man, but it's not what's going to happen." He gave the Messiah a crude wink. "But maybe I can help. The word is that one of your friends here is gonna rat you out to the Romans and they're going to nail you up on some kinda cross thing. If I can help you escape, I might save your hide."

"I've heard these rumors," the man told Hershel, "and I *have* got a plan. Maybe you can help me though, good sir. See, I've got this doppelganger stashed away by the police cells. He's a Roman guy who's dying anyway, a dead ringer for me if I may say so. The only problem is how me and my guys can somehow substitute his body for mine under the watchful eye of so many soldiers."

"I may be able to help," Hershel grinned. "Trust me, highness, I know what I'm doing."

THIRTY-ONE

At the evening's end, Jesus was happy to take wine from three or four different stone goblets, each of which he passed to Sten, who was acting as a restaurant busboy. Hershel, in the meantime, huddled with one of Jesus' men who avoided the Romans by denying that he knew the main man three times.

Mary went back to the cave where Hershel's time machine was stashed with Sten to wait. Hershel himself waited in the shadows outside the Roman barracks. When the soldiers arrested Jesus and brought him near, Hershel incanted a strong spell that left the soldiers giddy and confused while he and Jesus dragged the holy man's dying doppelganger into the cells then hurried away to the cave where Sten and Mary waited.

The Romans were somewhat confused the next morning with the weak and sick 'Jesus' they found in their captivity. His incoherent babbling along with his continued stumbling and dropping of the cross he was supposed to lug up the hill they wrote off as malingering, but with whips and shouts, they finally drove the exhausted alternate savior and his cross up the mountainside.

Cloaked by another spell conjured with all the skill both Merlin's possessed, Jesus and Mary stood by to witness the crucifixion. Jesus was, himself, appalled by the cruelty but glad to be apart from the scene which had been meant for him. Hershel suggested that they all head out of town for the weekend, maybe do a little fishing by the seashore. "After that, you might want to book passage for some distant land," Sten suggested more than once, "Someplace where you ain't so damn popular."

On the third day, the foursome returned to the cave where the body of Jesus' double had been buried. They used a spell of leverage Hershel had earlier perfected to roll back the heavy stone that sealed the tomb, and then had the real Jesus hide there in the cave until some followers came to pay their respects. When the worshipers approached, Jesus 'rose from the dead' to greet them, then quickly headed for the coast where a ship was waiting to take him and Mary to the distant land of Gaul, where the Romans hadn't yet established too much influence.

Sten and Hershel didn't hang around to wave goodbye as the ship pulled away from the shore. Their time machine was parked before Hershel's cave, where a nervous King Arthur paced and mumbled, before the Israeli ship had finished weighing anchor.

"Sten, man," Arthur shouted. "You were gone so long. What have you been up to?"

"Well, for one thing, we've got your Holy Grail," Hershel beamed. "In fact, we talked this Jesus guy into drinking wine from four different grails, just to be sure. One that we left there for the natives and three we brought back with us"

"Three Holy Grails?" King Irv chuckled. "That *is* a good marketing plan. Do you think we can sell all three?"

"Just covering our butts," Hershel grinned. "Besides, I've got some ideas about this grail thing, some other avenues where they might be popular."

"One of those guys back there was trying to convince us that we needed to bring back a whole long barbeque thing," Sten mumbled, "He said he was sure we were looking for the *Holy Grill*."

Arthur thought for a moment. "That might be worth something as well. Did you bring it with you?"

His question was met by dark looks from both Merlins. Just how much was this English king expecting of his loyal subjects? Even Sten was set to questioning what they were really doing here.

"Ah, highness," Sten asked, "why would you want an ancient barbeque grill? Even if it was five-hundred years old, how could you prove it to some Christian king that might have an interest in buying it?"

"I see your point," Arthur mused. "I guess we should just stick with these wine goblets then. Did this messiah fellow autograph these wine vessels or put some kind of authentication mark on them? Is there any easy way to prove they're genuine? I'm sure these other kings will be asking for some kind of pedigree when they ante up their cash"

"Your highness," Hershel spit at him. "We're dealing in ancient stolen artifacts here. If someone wants these things, they've got to have faith, just like they do in their whole religious belief thing. Are we supposed to be the catalyst for their beliefs? I think not! Either they believe us or they don't. If one group doesn't want this grail thing I'm sure another bunch will. We have to play on their desire for one-upmanship."

"One-upmanship?" King Irv chortled. "I never thought of it quite like that, but I think you've got something there. Just like the kingdom of Burton-on-Cherwell's fierce competition with Vaude to land the cathedral and the center of the Christian faith in our area."

"Exactly, your highness," Hershel told his king with a nod and a grin.

THIRTY-TWO

The war games were scheduled for the coming week end, so the two kings and their Merlins had little time to sit and discuss how they should proceed from here on the matter of the Holy Grail.

Sir Galahad and Sir Lancelot had worked King Arthur's men into a froth of frenzy. Anne of Rexia's ladies had trained just as hard, but retained an air of total cool about it. The gentlemen knights representing the kingdoms of Vaude and Wholesale knew they were prepared, so they made little show of practicing. The exercises they performed were hidden away to the east of Vaude, on the beaches of the North Sea.

At breakfast in the Warehouse Castle Saturday morning, Arthur made a very rude point of calling King Irv out and telling him that he would stand a scarce chance of winning anything at all.

"My men, just by their nature, are so far superior to your rag tag lot," Arthur bragged, "I've not seen a single one of your knights practicing their skills in our arena. Are they so confident that they've no need to further hone their skills? And the idea of lady knights even featuring in such a competition, well, what can I say?"

"We have an old saying around here," King Irv chuckled, "don't count your ducklings until they've hatched. And besides, my men stood very well against assailants from the future when they came in their own time machine to assault us."

"So what's that supposed to mean?" Arthur questioned. "What have ducks or future people got to do with the manly art of war?"

King Irv and all his people laughed at this. King Arthur had appeared to be smart and together, but as the going got tough...

"How about we just wait and see how these games of skill play out?" Irv asked. "If your men prove as superior as you've predicted, I will bow to you and give you all my kingdom's praises."

"All your kingdom's *praises*?" Arthur barked. "What does that mean?"

"Well, these are only games are they not?" The Jewish king reminded Arthur. "Were you expecting something more?"

Arthur gave a sort of choked cough. "No, my friend, forgive me, I seem to have gotten a bit carried away. You are right; these are only games of skill... So do you want to make a little wager on your fighting men?"

"I only want our dealing with this Christian grail thing to come off successfully," Irv told him. "That is why you approached me in the first place and that is what I agreed to help you with. These so-called 'manly games' are merely a way of passing time until we know where we stand with the marketing of the Holy Grail, which, by the way, we now have in our possession to work with. Is there a local contact you can speak with that will tell us just what this thing is worth?"

King Arthur fidgeted with the hem of his tunic, his eyes drifting around the room, avoiding King Irv's eyes.

"So there is no one locally," King Irv answered for him. "Here is what I propose. You take one of these wine goblets back to the west with you as soon as our games are finished. I'll have my Merlin, Hershel sign a letter of authentication which I will also sign myself. When you've found the highest bidder among your Christian contacts, I will trust you to send my share of the ransom, for indeed, ransom is about what this amounts to.

"In the meantime, I'll do what I can locally with one of the other Holy Grail cups. Hershel has some thoughts on that. The third grail cup, we will hold here in a sort of escrow against any future deals either of us might make. How does that sound?"

King Arthur took a long drink of his ale and drummed his fingertips on the arm of his chair for a few minutes before replying, "Okay, I guess that will work."

At about this time, Anne of Rexia entered the room. "I couldn't help but overhear what you were saying, highnesses. Forgive me, but I too have some interest in this Holy Grail thing. Your Merlins have brought back three such wine vessels. Should I not take one so that I may make my own deal with these crazy Christians that reside around my own realm? It would seem only fair."

"You, a woman?" burst forth from Arthur's lips. "From a kingdom, or whatever, run by women? Why should you be trusted to negotiate with anyone?"

King Irv put a hand on Arthur's sleeve. "My good regent," Irv told him. "It is not our place to judge. It would appear that our colleague Anne has a successful kingdom. She is entitled to our respect even though her beliefs might differ from our own."

"But women," Arthur sputtered. "Women who should be bearing and raising children, not defending the people who follow them…"

Anne rose up to her full height and stared dagger-like eyes at the western king. Irv thought that the two might actually come to blows until Arthur sort of melted back into the bench he was seated on.

"Tell you what," King Irv offered. "We're holding these games of skill today and tomorrow. How about you give Anne the chance to prove her prowess and that of her lady knights. If she can hold her own against your forces and mine we will grant her the third wine goblet that she can do her best with to make her own peace with the Christians that look down on her." Irv stared hard into Arthur's eyes, as if to tell him that he, Arthur, had better not be one of those casting aspersions on the lady ruler.

Arthur perked up at this suggestion. "Yes," he grinned, "I think that would be most fair," as he wrung his hands before him. "Shall we go up to the field of stones and let the games begin?"

THIRTY-THREE

Anne, Irv and Arthur emerged from Warehouse Castle to find all their troops and noble persons assembled just across the ninth green of King Irv's golf course, by the Warehouse Castle stables. The knights that were signed up to participate were decked out in full armor, while the others were bearing the standards of their various lands. It was a most colorful gathering, and it vibrated with the spirit of good, hearty competition.

Irv's son, Prince Sol, proudly held the white banner bearing a sky blue Star of David. One of Arthur's seconds leaned back on his steed to hold the green, red and white Pendragon flag aloft. Richard of Vaude held a light blue square of cloth with a golden cross superimposed over a darker blue Star of David to symbolize his kingdom's freedom of religion, the new flag they'd adopted after the death of his small-minded father, King John. The ladies of Rexia stood beneath a long pennant decorated with intertwined wildflowers over a bright yellow sun.

Sir Shecky leaned down confidently as King Irv walked by to give him a reassuring pat on the shoulder and a big smile. His body language told his king that their men couldn't be more ready for this event. Anne of Rexia stood tall in her saddle, wearing a broad, positive smile full of bright white teeth. Of all the monarchs, Anne alone chose to participate alongside her loyal subjects.

Arthur made a beeline for his people to seek their state of readiness, but none of his men took any notice. They were jeering and catcalling at their team leader, Sir Lancelot, who pranced up and down on his sorrel steed trying to secure the attention of Queen Guinevere. King Arthur's face turned a deep shade of crimson as he walked by his men, pretending to have some further destination in mind with his stroll.

King Richard of Vaude, although he was not on the schedule to participate, sat on a tall buttermilk stallion before his own brave fighters. The noble representatives of Vaude sat at attention behind their king with serious faces that said 'we already know that victory is ours.'

At a signal from King Irv, the parade to the fairgrounds formed up with the knights of Wholesale leading the procession, followed by King Richard and the men of Vaude. Sir Lancelot and Arthur's knights followed next, with Lancelot weaving and preening before his men. Guinevere was nowhere in sight, but it could be well assumed that she was somewhere nearby, watching her lover making a spectacle of himself.

The lady contestants of Rexia brought up the rear. Anne sat astride a white mare of at least fourteen hands, her head held high. The female warriors behind her showed stern and dedicated faces under the lifted visors of their helmets.

The parade entered the King's Highway just west of Warehouse Castle and marched north, past the golf course and the roadside attraction. At the field of stones, they turned east to the Wholesale fairgrounds where they found an oval racetrack and a broad field set up for the games in its center. A temporary grandstand was in front complete with upper level boxes for each competing group's leader. Queen Sophie was fussing about King Irv's area, with a few lady friends that she'd invited as her special guests. Hershel sat in the back row, a small keg of ale beside him for himself and his regent. Prince Sol's wife, Amy, who had given over her life to Jesus after her mother died, would not attend any such heathen event. If anyone should be looking, she could be found at the cathedral in Vaude, praying for her husband's salvation.

Arthur's box held only his Merlin, Sten, and Guinevere, who leaned over the front rail to watch for Lancelot's approach. The Rexia booth was empty as was the Vaude space.

The day began with a horse race around the marked-off and barricaded oval. King Irv's groundskeepers had said that the circumference of the track measured approximately two and a half miles as it encircled all the other event areas.

Anne herself chose to represent her group. Arthur started to protest that both the lady and her horse were so large they would have a big advantage, but Irv silenced him with a glare.

Arthur's choice was Sir Bors de Ganis, the smallest and lightest of all his round-table fellows. His logic was the man was so light of weight that the horse would hardly notice him and therefore wouldn't be burdened down. Irv's son, Prince Sol, an exceptional horseman all his young life, strode out to represent the Wholesale Kingdom.

At the last minute, King Richard had a change of heart and substituted his youngest knight, Sir Baxter, for his first choice jockey, Sir Wilfred. Baxter appeared nervous as he mounted his gray gelding. This would be his first appearance in public representing his king.

The horses walked up to the starting gate, took their places and waited until Queen Sophie, high up in Irv's box, dropped her handkerchief and someone gave a loud whistle. Three horses shot from the gate. Baxter's mount hesitated a few seconds, but as the young man dug in his spurs, the horse charged forward, quickly passing the others. Baxter's horse, Sally, held the lead more than halfway around the track, the others bunched close on his heels, when Queen Anne sounded a loud war whoop and barreled past like a cannon shot.

Sir Bors de Ganis raised up in his saddle, wielding a short crop from side to side in an effort to fire up his mount, but to no avail. Prince Sol's poor horse looked around in confusion, ready to quit running and head for the stables.

"Oy, that son of yours." Sophie scolded. "*Our* son," Irv reminded her. "And I believe he's doing his best. He just needs a little Mahzel." Sophie put her palms over her eyes. "Okay, but I can't bear to watch this."

In the end, Anne crossed the finish line a good two lengths ahead of Baxter and Sally. Arthur started to renew his protest that Anne and her ride had an unfair advantage in their size, but the judges weren't hearing any of it.

THIRTY-FOUR

The next event was jousting. Sir Lancelot, insisting that he lead off for King Arthur, and not taking Queen Anne as a serious threat, was unseated twice before he started concentrating and finally fought her to a draw on their third attempt.

Next, Sir Wilfred stood for King Richard against Irv's Sir Ibraham. The two were old friends, each knowing well the other's strengths and weak points. Twice they battled to a draw, breaking their lances against each other's shields. On their third try, Ibraham freighted left with his pole, then came around, catching his buddy off guard. Wilfred, surprised by the quick move and brutally knocked from his mount, decided to be extra vigilant for the last rounds and managed to unseat Ibraham in two succeeding charges, placing Wilfred against Anne for the final rounds.

On their first pass, Wilfred went easy on Anne, because, he reasoned, she was a lady. She knocked him off his mount and onto his rear so hard the man almost lost consciousness. As Wilfred shook the stars from his head and remounted his horse, he told himself not to be so naive in the future. Wilfred never succeeded in unseating the female queen, but at least he managed to hold his own, losing only on points.

In the hand to hand combat with swords everyone had a good laugh when Anne's second in command, Lady Oprah, fought Sir Lancelot into a corner. When Lance had his back against the boards, Lady Oprah leaned in close and softly said, "Does my bum look big in this outfit?" half-turning from the man.

Lancelot, always the ladies man, leaned forward to look around at the lady knight's backside, at which time she slapped his sword-bearing wrist with the flat of her blade. Lance cried out and dropped his weapon, after which Lady Oprah launched a merciless attack, totally destroying the shield of Arthur's top knight.

This pattern continued throughout the day, leaving Rexia far ahead on points with Vaude in a strong second place. Arthur sat in his special section, watching his queen who was watching intently after every move Lancelot made. He drank pint after pint of strong ale. When the ale keg ran dry, Arthur found a bottle of brandy. He spent the afternoon drinking, glaring at his lady and following the contests with one eye. He vowed to himself that he would conjure up some excuse to accuse Lancelot of treason and have his manhood removed and fed to the pigs.

THIRTY-FIVE

By the end of the day, Sunday, it was clear that Anne's lady knights knew their stuff. They had taken the top prizes in more than half the contests of skill and stamina. While Arthur's men strutted up to each event like proud peacocks, they seemed to have no endurance in the long run. The noblemen of Wholesale and Vaude held their own very well against all comers, taking the majority of the remaining honors after Rexia.

Arthur's top man, Lancelot, King Irv observed, was constantly glancing over at Arthur's good queen, Guinevere, and showing off to her as if her approval was the only thing that mattered across the various events. More than once he was tossed from the saddle while his attention was divided between game and lady. Arthur was only too aware of what was going on and seemed to be seething in his royal viewing box. The western king had consumed too much drink as he glanced back and forth between the arena and the woman sitting at his side.

Sunday evening's banquet found Arthur unable to hold up his head or speak a coherent sentence as he watched his queen and his top knight making eyes at each other across the table, Lancelot licking meat juice from between a V formed of his first and middle fingers and Guinevere responding by circling her own tongue around her full, red lips. Just after the second course arrived, the western king stood on unsteady legs and called out to Guinevere that they were leaving the dinner. "I'm tired and have no appetite," he mumbled before taking her hand and pulling the lady from her seat. He was further embarrassed exiting the hall as his lady turned to blow a kiss in Sir Lancelot's direction.

A ripple of laughter ran through the others of Arthur's entourage to further embarrass him as they climbed the stairs. Was the cuckolded husband always the last to know? He wished he could grab his grail cup and leave right now, under the cover of darkness.

Monday morning found a rather green-gilled King Arthur swaying in his saddle as he bid farewell to King Irv and Queen Sophie, thanking them for their hospitality and making a special point of praising Hershel for all his help. As the king's entourage passed out onto the King's Highway, a grinning Sir Lancelot led the troops behind king and queen, wearing a big, nasty grin and doffing his hat to those watching the departure. The man appeared to have neither shame nor couth.

"Oy, that poor man," Queen Sophie lamented when the parade had passed. "Arthur seems too nice a fellow to have such an unfaithful wife as that. He should have all his knights study the Torah and learn how to behave, morally, I mean." Irv nodded his agreement, thinking there must be something more to this picture that we're not seeing.

Irv's own knight, Sir Ibraham, seemed to be reading his thoughts as they walked back toward Warehouse Castle. "It's this Christian thing," he said, laying a hand on Irv's shoulder. "I'm not a nosy man, but I heard some talk among that man's soldiers."

Queen Sophie's face brightened. "Really?" she asked. "Not that I'm interested in gossip or anything, but please, tell us what you overheard."

"Well..." Sir Ibraham hesitated.

"Might as well go ahead and tell all," Irv demurred. "It couldn't bring any more harm than's already been done."

"Well," Ibraham began again. "The word is that good Queen Guinevere has secretly gone over to the Christians. She's a follower of some crazy Irish monk who calls himself Patrick. Lancelot, who has had the hots for Guinevere for some time, pardon my language, my good lady queen, he went to this Patrick and joined the church as well in a move to win the queen's heart. Guinevere has been denying Arthur his husbandly rights for some time because he *isn't* a Christian and good Christian Lancelot has been filling in for him. That's part of this whole 'search for the grail' wheeze. Arthur thinks he can bargain with this Patrick fellow to get him to release his hold on Queen Guinevere in trade for the Holy Grail."

"Ack, what a sad story," Sophie lamented. "And she seemed like such a nice girl."

"Never mind," Irv told her, patting her hand. "We've got our own grail to figure out and I don't think Friar Agnello is going to be interested in it. I've got to talk with Hershel and see where he sees us going with this thing. Mark my words, I've got a gut feeling that we won't hear anything more from good King Arthur, which is to say, he probably won't pay a shackle of what he owes me in this matter."

THIRTY-SIX

Later that morning, Hershel saw his monarch approaching the Merlin's cave. He ducked back inside, grabbed a couple tankards and had a fresh ale waiting when Irv had crossed the golf course and arrived at his door.

"Hershel, Hershel," King Irv began. "We have this Holy Grail thing. Arthur says that all the Christians want it, but I haven't seen any evidence of that. So how do we make some money off this thing?"

"I've been giving that some thought," Hershel answered with a confident look. "It probably ain't just Christian folks in *our* time who are interested in this. Remember, in the future time where Princess Judith and Rutherford live, there's still plenty of Christians, probably a lot more than in our time."

"Yes," King Irv replied with some curiosity. "So we'll travel to the future and sell it?"

"Nah," Hershel scoffed, "more like rent it."

"*Rent* it?" his confused king parroted.

"Yeah, kinda," Hershel chortled. "Ralph is always looking for ways to promote the brewery out there in the future. How about we ask Rutherford to organize some kind of special tour for the Holy Grail? These future people have plenty of money to spend and they like to see all kinds of weird things. We'll have Rutherford arrange to send the Holy Grail on a tour all around the world, sponsored by Ralph's Metaphysical Brewing Company of San Francisco. Any church or museum that wants to display the grail for a month or more will give Ralph a percentage of the price they charge for admission, and Ralph will pass it on to Rutherford, who'll send most of it to us, or at least put it in our future Barclay's Bank account."

"And what, pray tell, does Ralph get out of all this?" Irv asked.

"Are you kidding?" Hershel exploded, "only the greatest kind of publicity in the world. Ralph's Metaphysical Brewing Company will be on people's lips all over the globe, and soon his ale will be as well. What better advertising could you get at any price? And when Ralph's milked the thing for all it's worth, we can bring it back here and flog it off to someone for another small amount of gold. It's a win-win situation, highness."

King Irv took a moment to ponder this. "I'm just a simple country king," he told his Merlin, "but why don't you run this by Rutherford and maybe Ralph as well. If they like the idea, well, it'll be a lot easier than trying to beg for gold from the local Christian cathedrals around here.

Hershel was back from future England within a couple days, even before the week had finished. "Irv," he told his king, "You won't believe how excited both Ralph and Rutherford are over this idea. Ralph says he loves it because he always wanted to stick a finger in the eye of the church, along with the money he knows he can make off all this publicity. He's thinking he might even open a few more breweries around the world on the strength of this, like maybe in China or Eastern Europe.

"Rutherford, who you'll remember is Jewish like we are, is looking at it strictly as a financial coup, I think that's what he called it. He told me there're still religions that take a dim view of drinking ale or any alcoholic beverage, and this might be just the gesture that will make them re-evaluate their thoughts about beer. Could ale or beer be all that bad if it's bringing the cup that their savior drank wine from to them? It also dispels their idea that their savior was against drinking, as they'll have to admit that he was drinking wine.

"That's a lot to ponder," King Irv told him. "We certainly seem to be a factor in the future world's history. If only there was a way we could use this to make Judaism more popular in the future world."

"One thing at a time, highness," Hershel winked. "You never know where all this could lead us."

"Yes, you're a wise man, Hershel," King Irv replied as he lifted his tankard for another drink. "I think we may have a good thing going here."

THIRTY-SEVEN

Hershel made another trip in his time machine two days later, this time going directly to San Francisco where he passed the Holy Grail to Ralph at the Metaphysical Brewing Company. Seated at the bar, he slowly and carefully unwrapped the old wine goblet with a big grin and exclaimed, "Ta-dah."

Ralph squinted at the plain clay cup, picked it up for a closer inspection with one eye closed, then put it back on the bar saying, "That's it?"

"Well, I mean, it's from a long time back in history," Hershel told him apologetically. "What did they have back then? Certainly no big wineries that could afford to make custom stem glasses with fancy logos on them."

"Yeah," Ralph replied slyly, "But isn't the Holy Grail supposed to be encrusted with gold, jewels and other baubles? When my old mum used to drag me to church, they made a big thing every Easter about how spectacular and exceptional was the cup Jesus drank from. I mean, this looks like something you could buy at some Navaho souvenir stand out on the Arizona desert. Isn't there some way we could spruce it up a little? Make it look more authentic?"

"What's more authentic?" Hershel asked him with a serious face. "I grabbed it from right under this Jesus guy's nose. If someone could take finger prints off the thing, they'd find this savior's prints all over it... if they have any record of the guy's fingerprints."

"Which, of course, they don't," Ralph barked, "unless they've got some secret police file deep in the bowels of the Vatican in Rome."

"So, do you want to organize a tour for the thing or not?" Hershel asked. "Cause if you don't, I'll just take it back with me and we'll flog it off to some unsuspecting Christian group in our own time."

Ralph thought for a minute, his brow creased, and finally answered, "Let's not be hasty here. I've got a good PR team working for me. I'm sure they can put an acceptable spin on it. Maybe we can borrow some other Christian relics, even real authentic ones, to make this tour thing a 'must see' event. Just leave it with me. I'll give Rutherford a call tonight and set things rolling."

"You're sure," said a hesitant Hershel.

"Trust me," Ralph grinned, putting an arm across the Merlin's shoulders. "I know what I'm doing."

Hershel got a room down the street at the Motel 8, deciding that, as long as he was here, he'd rent a car and spend some time at the beach, maybe head north to the Napa wine country. It was always a nice break from the monotony of life in old England. He enjoyed all the young ladies who sunbathed along Bodega Bay without their tops, so different from the stuffy old Wholesale Kingdom.

He spent the following day taking his time on a leisurely drive north, stopping for a few pints and lunch at the Pelican Inn in Marin County, and then strolling along the lovely California coastline. By nightfall, he had a room at the inn in Napa and a couple of jugs of Cabernet wine.

Hershel met an older lady who had singled him out in the Edward's Wine Store and asked if they could take a walk along the river to have some time to talk and get to know each other. The Merlin had invited her to his motel room to watch something called a movie on the motel's television.

The next day, driving back to Berkeley to retrieve his time machine, Hershel couldn't remember a thing about the so-called movie. What he did retain were wonderful cameos of the California lady who was so nice to him. She gave him an hour long massage before she rolled him over and made slow passionate love to him. He almost wished he lived in this future land where people were so free and willing to share intimacy… almost.

"But I can always come back here to visit this place and its wonderful people," he assured himself as he checked in his rental and went to retrieve his time machine, this time disguised as an Alfa Romeo roadster, in the back lot of Ralph's Metaphysical Brewing Company.

As he was getting into his time travel contraption to head back through time, he heard Ralph calling his name.

"Hershel, hey, Hershel, wait."

The Merlin stepped out of his machine and stood, waiting for his friend to approach. "So what's going on, Ralph," he called.

"We've got a deal," the brewer shouted back. "Come on inside, have an ale with me and I'll explain it all to you."

Hesitantly, Hershel left his time travel thingy, still disguised as the latest Alfa Romeo model, and walked toward the back door of the brewery. "What kinda deal?" he called out.

As the Merlin reached the brewery's back door, Ralph threw an arm around his shoulder and guided him upstairs to the small special events room. Rutherford was seated at the table along with three other men Hershel didn't recognize. In the middle of the table sat the so-called Holy Grail, although at first, Hershel didn't recognize it.

The simple clay vessel now sported an assortment of rubies, opals and other bright gem stones. On one side there was a small cross of what appeared to be solid gold. The cup had been fired in a kiln so that now it shown with a bright glaze.

"You mentioned that we might spruce it up a bit," Ralph told him. "So what do you think?"

"A cross?" Hershel countered. "When this messiah guy drank from the thing he hadn't been hung on any cross yet. What gives here?"

"A small bit of minutia," one of the PR men at the table chuckled. "These Christian folks get very emotional about this 'cross' symbol. No one will be concerned that this Last Supper wheeze occurred before their so-called crucifixion. The cross will be a sort of affirmation that this is truly the Holy Grail."

"Are you sure about this?" Hershel mumbled incredulously. "I mean, are these folks all total idiots?"

"That's the beauty of the scam," one of the others at the table beamed.

"So, Hershel," Ralph said with a suddenly serious face, "Do you want to make some money on this thing or not? 'Cause I certainly want all this free publicity."

King Irv and the Holy Grail

As Hershel looked around, all the eyes were focused directly on him. "Well, King Irv did kinda imply..."

"Great," Ralph answered loudly. "Then it's settled. The tour will begin the first of June right here in San Francisco, at our Museum of Natural History. From here we'll send the thing to Los Angeles and then eastward to Chicago and New York, Europe after that. This is going to be just too great, too immense!"

Hershel kinda shrunk back into his plush leather chair. What had he unleashed? "I guess I'd better get back and let King Irv know about all this," he said. When he'd finished his ale and another after it, he told them, "I should probably be going to share all this good news with the King right away."

⚜ THIRTY-EIGHT ⚜

"**B**ut that sounds very deceptive," King Irv told Hershel. "Is this how we want to conduct business?"

"That's why I wanted to talk to you, your highness. Ralph, Rutherford, and all their people seem to think it's cool, but it seems kinda hinky to me. Maybe we should have a talk with Rabbi Weiss."

"And are you ready to explain all this to the good Rabbi?" Irv asked his Merlin. "Like how you went back in time and got this Jesus fellow to give you not one, but three such wine vessels? If so, you're a braver man than I am. How about we just let time take its course? At least we'll be getting some return on our investment."

"If you say so, Irv," Hershel replied. "So how about we have a pint of ale while we think about it?"

"I thought we just decided…"

"Yeah, your highness," Hershel told him, "but I'll sleep better on our decision after we've had a bit to drink."

"Hershel," King Irv chuckled, "you *do* have a conscience. I admire that in a man. But I trust Rutherford's thinking, even if I'm a little unsure of our friend Ralph."

"Unsure of Ralph how?" Queen Sophie asked, entering the hall. "Is he welshing on his agreement with us and Rutherford?"

"No, my good lady," Irv smiled, getting up and pulling out a chair for his wife. "We're talking about something completely different."

"It's this Holy Grail business, isn't it?" she spit at them, folding her arms across her chest. "I knew this wouldn't come to anything good."

"Sophie, my dear," Irv soothed. "Everything is just fine. There's no problem with Rutherford or Ralph…"

"It's just what? I can hear something in your tone of voice, husband. You might as well tell momma all about it."

While King Irv stared at the toes of his boots, Hershel decided to speak up. "Rutherford will be sending our Holy Grail thing all around the future world, just as we talked about," he told her. "It's just that he, uh, they, well…"

"They've ruined the thing," Irv thundered, finally finding his voice. "They've dressed it up like putting lipstick on a pig, adding the jewels and baubles that they believe most future Christians would expect to see on it. They've even added a gold cross. They've ruined the authenticity! And I can say that even though I'm not a Christian and wouldn't want to be one."

"Oh, husband," Queen Sophie laughed. "Why should we care as long as we're making some money on this deal? You've said yourself that we'll probably never see a sou from that King Arthur fellow. Hasn't Rutherford always been good to us financially? If it seems right to him, who are we to question?"

Irv gave a searching look at his wife. Hershel raised his flagon to signal the serving staff that they needed more ale. When Wendy appeared, Sophie said, "You'd better bring some wine for me as well."

Over their drinks, Queen Sophie scolded her husband. "It is the same Holy Grail that this savior fellow drank from, right?" Irv and Hershel both nodded agreement.

"So we've tarted it up a bit, what's the harm? It's still the item they are paying money to see, is it not?" Irv and Hershel both nodded agreement again.

"So where's the harm?" Queen Sophie asked them in a stern voice. "And I'm sure the Rabbi would agree with me, though I can understand why you don't want to solicit his opinion on this matter."

Hershel lightly punched Irv's shoulder with his fist. "Highness, I believe you have one very smart wife."

King Irv's face broke out in a wide grin. "I believe you are right, Hershel. She is one in a million." He rose from his chair and went over to give his Sophie a big hug and a kiss. "Our little secret, this," he whispered in her ear. "If things go wrong, we'll deny all knowledge."

But in the following weeks, all reports from the future were very positive. According to Rutherford, people had been lined up around the block in both San Francisco and Los Angeles to have a glimpse of the ancient relic. Chicago reported that they had already sold out their first scheduled week of showing. The Holy Grail was a huge box-office success and more venues around the world were clamoring for the opportunity to display the thing. Rutherford reported that it looked like their Holy Grail vessel would be circulating for a good three years or more.

THIRTY-NINE

A s the Holy Grail's popularity was cresting across the future world, King Arthur appeared on Irv's doorstep with a small pin to burst the bubble.

"Hey, Ace," he shouted when Irv greeted him at the gate. "I think you and your so-called Merlin have some s'plainin' to do."

"Nice to see you, too," King Irv replied graciously. "So, what is the problem that you bring to my humble kingdom?"

"It's that damned so-called Holy Grail," the western king screamed, his face as red as a ripe apple and his breath coming in short rasps. "I think your Merlin sold me a bill of goods. All the Christians in my area are laughing at me. That damned Irishman, Patrick, told me it looked like something an amateur artist spun on a potter's wheel in a drunken fit. I want my money back."

King Irv had to chuckle at this. "But you haven't, as yet, given me any money. I've been expecting some kind of remuneration from you over the past months. After all, we did enter into this venture together. My Merlin did his part…"

"Total deception," the western king shouted. "He probably paid some child to fashion this grail thing."

"Your own man, Sten, was by Hershel's side when the so-called savior gave them the vessel…"

"Sten," Arthur snarled. "He's not done a lick of work since we returned from your castle to our homeland. Every morning he's down to the beach with some crazy wooden board that he's fashioned, and he has half my knights with him. They say they're surfing, whatever that means? Surfing!"

"If you come in, calm down, and have an ale with Hershel and myself, maybe we can try to figure out what you're doing wrong in your approach to these Christian folks. Our own Holy Grail has gained amazing acceptance all over the future world. We are doing quite well with it."

This revelation only seemed to further enflame Arthur's anger. Irv's further question regarding the good health of his good queen was like gasoline on the flames.

"Guinevere has run off to Ireland with that no-good Lancelot," Arthur wailed with tears in his eyes. "Everything I've worked for all these many years is lost. My life seems hopeless!"

With great empathy, King Irv told the man, "Please come inside. Let me fetch you an ale. You seem to be most distraught. Are your good knights here with you?"

"Only a handful," King Arthur fired back with tears in his eyes, "Just the most loyal. Lancelot has turned many of my men against me, feeding them the words of this Bible thing and telling them that I'm the devil incarnate, does that make any sense?"

"I'm not familiar with these Christian beliefs," Irv answered him, straight faced. "But that would certainly be one method of trying to overthrow your rule. We'll have to consult with Hershel in these matters. I'm sure he can come up with some sort of remedy."

"This Patrick fellow keeps returning to our Cornish shores and preaching to my men who are down on the beach with their surfing. How can I defend my kingdom when the very men assigned to the task are being corrupted by my enemy? And with words! No one has, as yet, raised a hand in violence."

"Yes, this will require great thought," King Irv answered, massaging his temples with his left thumb and fore finger.

The two men sat in silence for some time, finishing their first pint and starting a second that Wendy quickly brought them when she noticed that they were getting low on drink. Midway through their second ale, Hershel entered the hall.

"Majesty? I didn't know we had company. Hey, Arthur, is Sten here with you?"

King Arthur seemed to choke on an intake of breath, his face glowing red again before he answered King Irv's Merlin.

"I'm fed up with Sten," he barked. "I'm going to be advertising for a new Merlin soon. All Sten ever does is hang out on the beach with some of my rebellious knights and something he calls a surfboard."

Hershel took a step back, feeling guilty that he'd turned Sten's attention to surfing so that he'd quit staring at the bathing beauties on the beach by San Francisco.

Rearing back on his heels, Hershel announced, "Well, that's pretty rude, your highness. We'd never tolerate such a thing here in Wholesale."

King Irv had to chortle to himself at this outburst from his Merlin. He knew that his own knights would never be so insubordinate. He treated his people right and they all returned the favor.

"Arthur, my man," Irv finally spoke, "could there be some other underlying reasons why your men are displeased with you? I don't mean to question your leadership abilities, but could there be something amiss within your organization?"

"That upstart Lancelot having the hots for my good lady for a start," Arthur fired back.

"Yes, I get that," Irv told him. "And I'm not sure exactly how we can cool the ardor of one randy knight, but I'm sure there are other things you can do. You say this Christian Patrick finds your good men on the beach? How about if you move your seat of government east, away from the ocean shores?"

"Abandon Tintagel?" came Arthur's horrified reply. "But our family have always lived there. Where else could we possibly go?"

"Are there not unclaimed lands to the east of you? You could still maintain rule over Tintagel and the Cornish coast, but from some nearby inland place. That would keep your knights off the beach and make it more difficult for this Patrick menace to approach your people. How about you stake out a new center for your rule? You can give it a catchy name like, maybe, Camelot."

"I'll have to give that some thought," Arthur answered with some confusion. "It might be nice to make a new start, especially if I could get Guinevere's attention away from this Christian business."

"Well, give it some thought," Irv counseled. "You're welcome to stay here for a fortnight or so while you get things together in your head. And Hershel will give what counsel he might while you're here. My Merlin is quite the man of the world and therefore very knowledgeable."

King Irv and the Holy Grail

King Arthur fell back into one of Irv's divans, totally deflated, and closed his eyes. When Irv returned hours later, Arthur was still in a deep sleep. "The man must have been exhausted," Irv told his tabby cat, Bird.

FORTY

When Arthur crossed the golf course the next morning, he found Hershel's time machine, as well as the man himself, gone. Wendy, the serving wench, approached the Cornish king when he returned to Warehouse Castle from the Merlin's cave.

"Hershel left this note for you, highness," she told him with a deep curtsey. "He said he would be back in a few days and you should make yourself at home and relax until his return. He hopes to have some answers for you from the future. Can I bring you an ale?"

Arthur dithered for a few seconds, finally voicing, "Yes, an ale would be fine. Is King Irv up yet?"

"I'm afraid he's out on the golf course with his son, the king of Vaude and the Rabbi," she apologized. "They usually return in time for what Irv calls his 'liquid lunch,' just past midday," she giggled.

"I've nothing better to do than wait," Arthur frowned. "Just keep the ale coming. I'll be seated outside on the bailey."

The foursome returned from the links to find King Arthur, arms and legs akimbo, sprawled out on a fat, cushioned chair, snoring. He had a nearly empty ale vessel on the table in front of him along with the note Hershel had left. The missive from the Merlin basically told Arthur that he, Hershel, would return soon with statistics about how well their Holy Grail vessel was being received by the people of the future. "I'll be joining our world tour team at the British Museum in London to gather all the information I can from King Irv's son-in-law, who organized the tour," his message concluded.

As the golfers took their seats around the table, Arthur popped open one less-than-friendly eye to take them all in. After a minute, he shook his head and tried to smile. "King Irv, King Richard, Rabbi, I'm sorry, I seemed to have dozed off. What time is it?"

King Richard laughed at this. "It's time you had another pint of ale," he ventured. "We are all just about to put in our order."

"Wendy," the Rabbi called. "Do we have some ale and maybe a glass of Cabernet wine handy?"

The serving wench was right there to answer his call, "Three ales and a wine?"

Arthur raised his mug and dramatically let the last golden drop fall to his extended tongue. "Make that four ales," he barked. Wendy giggled and turned to head back into the castle.

"So what brings you back to our fair land?" King Richard asked Arthur.

"King Arthur is having some trouble flogging off his Holy Grail vessel to the church folks in his area," Irv announced. "They seem to believe the thing's too simple to be authentic. They don't seem to realize that it is simply elegant."

"That's these Christians for you," the Rabbi smiled with a nod of his head. "Always expecting too much and never satisfied."

King Irv and the Holy Grail

"Let's be fair now," King Richard replied. "These ancient vessels *are* rather plain. Hardly fitting of the legend His followers have created around this so-called savior fellow. What should we expect?"

"Not our circus, not our monkeys," King Irv answered, lifting his flagon to take a deep draught of ale. "But you should know, good Arthur," Irv continued after he swallowed his drink, "that my friends in the future did dress up their vessel a little. They pasted on some gemstones and a golden cross. Would it be too late for you to do something similar?"

"That sounds a bit deceptive," Arthur told them with a skeptical face, which quickly broke into a grin. "I'm all for it. Where do I begin?"

"Wait until Hershel returns," Irv told him. "My clever Merlin has the answers. And from what he might be learning in future England as we speak, he might have even more ideas."

Arthur took another drink, then said, "You know, I tried to explain to them that in his time, this savior was just some ordinary man!"

"And how did they answer that?" the Rabbi asked.

"They called me a Blasphemer! 'How could you say such a thing,' they shouted." King Arthur screwed up his face and cringed at the memory. "What is a blasphemer, anyway?"

FORTY-ONE

"I hope King Irv won't be upset," Rutherford told Hershel as they sat in the snack bar of the British Museum sipping tea. "I found a small company in China that's provided us with five-thousand small replicas of this Holy Grail thing, authentic in every detail including, of course, what we added. The miniature grails are on sale in the gift shop here for the equivalent of $19.95 each and selling well. There are even some tiny ones attached to key chains at $5.99.

"We've shipped some to the museums in California, Chicago and New York where I understand people are buying them in droves even though the exhibit has moved on from there."

"I don't think anything is gonna upset King Irv as long as we're making a few shekels off it." Hershel leered. "So I noticed you've got quite a line of people waiting to get in to see this…"

"At ten pounds a head," Rutherford grinned. "The museum people are very pleased. This Holy Grail exhibit will finance a lot of serious archeological work for them in the Holy Land and other places. They're considering us a God-send."

"So why is King Arthur having so much trouble getting anyone to listen in our own, I mean, in our past times?"

"Probably something to do with the level of education," Rutherford surmised. "Most these museum patrons have modern advanced university degrees, unlike either the peasants or the clergy in the time of Irving and Arthur. Plus the fact that we've tarted the thing up a bit with costume jewelry and a golden cross."

"Yeah," Hershel said. "That costume jewelry thing adds a lot…"

"How about if this King Arthur goes back to his people and accuses someone of trying to steal the gem stones from the grail? He can add a few precious stones along with a small cross to the thing, saying that he was restoring what was there originally when it was brought to him, and find someone to scapegoat for denuding the thing after it was found?"

"A scapegoat would have to pay a pretty heavy price for such a thing," Hershel gave with a worried face.

"It doesn't have to be a real person," Rutherford told him with a look. "Say it was someone on the other side of the island who has been made to pay the price by some other king. I know these peasants love the sight of blood, but if you can describe it realistically enough…"

"Yeah, that might just do," Hershel replied, rolling his eyes upward. "That's a good first plan. So what's our backup position?"

"Like, maybe we didn't trust showing them the grail with all the gemstones because we didn't trust them not to defile the thing? I don't know. From what I've read of this part of English history, nobody trusted anyone else anyway, kings suspected kings, church people suspected other church people."

"I'll take that under consideration," Hershel replied, "but I don't think King Irv would be too happy with the idea. He runs a pretty open and up-front kingdom, ruling by what the Rabbi has taught him from the Torah."

FORTY-TWO

Hershel returned to Wholesale to find King Arthur pacing outside his cave. "So what have you found?" the western monarch demanded in a loud voice, approaching the Merlin's time machine without so much as a 'how do you do?' to greet the man.

Unsure of just how to answer, Hershel offered Arthur a seat at his small table and a pint of ale. "I've just traveled across some fourteen hundred years, your majesty," Hershel told him. "You'll have to let me sit back and gather my thoughts before you start accosting me with tough questions."

"Tough questions?" Arthur barked in his face. "I merely inquired as to what you might have found in this future place."

"And you've never *been* to this 'future place,' have you?" Hershel spit back at him. "You have no idea what it's like. It's much more crowded and complicated than our kingdom or your own."

King Arthur took a step back. "I'm sorry, good sir, I had no idea."

"You bet your sweet bippy you haven't," Hershel fired back suppressing a grin, "so just chill for a moment while I grab us each a drink. After I've had a chance to unwind a bit, I'll share it all with you."

King Arthur sat, but couldn't hide his restlessness. His knees bounced, his fingers drummed and his head moved to some unheard tune. Hershel sported a straight face, but behind his calm look, he was laughing at this king who wore his emotions so blatantly.

Finally, as Hershel poured their second drinks, he said, "Highness, you won't believe how popular our Holy Grail thing is among the folks in the future. People are lined up around the block at the museums where we're showing it. Christian church people are lining up as well to testify to its authenticity. There are very few doubters among these future Christians."

A long growl of frustration escaped from King Arthur's lips. "Why must I be faced with such doubting Thomas's?" he cried. "I only want to win back the love of my wife and get these Christian folk off my back!"

"Keep the faith," Hershel told him with a sly wink. "All is not lost, yet. We've still got some easy options, and if they fail, we could always try a bit of magic. I'm surprised Sten hasn't proposed some of this magic thing to you."

"Sten," Arthur wailed. "Don't mention that name to me. That worthless magician only wants to paddle out into the sea off our Tintagel Castle and try to ride back to shore on the waves. I'm coming to hate that man and this surfing wheeze as well."

Hershel tried hard to suppress a wave of guilt for his part in introducing Sten to surfing off the coast of San Francisco. "Highness?" he fired back. "Maybe I need to return to this Tintagel place with you and have a heart-to-heart with Sten. We men of magic tend to understand each other better than, say, folks of noble birth do. I could speak with Sten and try to steer him to a better course."

"That's fine," Arthur lamented with a tear in his eye, "But how can that bring back the love of my lady, Guinevere? Do you possibly have a spell to render my unfaithful knight, Lancelot, impotent so that my lady's affection might be turned back toward me?"

"Irv," Hershel pleaded with his friend and king. "I really don't want to travel to the west coast with this crazy king. I ain't 'Dear Abbey,' you know. I mean that's why his kingdom has a Merlin in the first place."

"So why are you even thinking about such a journey?" his perplexed king asked.

"Well…" Hershel pondered. "I guess I feel a bit guilty. In future San Francisco Sten was embarrassing me. He was staring at the future people and their mode of dress, some of which I'll admit was pretty revealing. To get his mind off the bodies of the young girls, I pointed out the surfers. Somehow, Sten got hooked on the idea of riding a surfboard into the shore. So what do I do now?"

"Don't tell anyone this," King Irv chuckled. "If Arthur or his people should ask, deny any knowledge. We can't be responsible for the foibles of our neighbors."

"But if Sten should say…"

"Deny, Hershel, deny. No one was there to witness anything and you are not your brother's keeper."

"If you say so, highness."

"Damn straight," Irv told him, lifting his mug for another drink. "But, on the other hand, we *do* need to figure a way that we can help Arthur sell his copy of the Holy Grail to the people of the west. I would venture to say it's the only way we'll ever be shut of him." King Irv wiped his mouth on the sleeve of his robe and held his mug out for a refill.

"Did I tell you about the tchotchkes that Rutherford is selling everywhere they show the grail thing? They've made some miniature models of the cup that people are going crazy for. Tiny Holy Grail replicas, they're amazing."

"Well, that should lend some sort of credibility," King Irv chuckled. "The good people of our lands are the ultimate judges. Have you told Arthur about this?"

"I did, your highness, but it just sent him off on a tangent about his unfaithful wife."

King Irv gave a series of 'Tsks" and shook his head. "I wish I'd never met that man," the Wholesale monarch confessed.

![dragon] FORTY-THREE ![dragon]

"**S**o are you coming west with me?" Arthur asked Hershel that evening over supper at Warehouse Castle. "My entourage is almost ready to hit the hot and dusty, probably Friday at the latest."

Hershel gave a pleading glance at his king. "I'm really a very poor traveler," he confessed.

"Nonsense," Arthur barked. "You go all over the world, back and forth through time. Is this not traveling?"

"Well," Hershel threw back at him, "Time travel is a bit different. I'm here one minute and I'm there the next. I don't have to spend days astride a horse or nights sleeping on the ground among all the fleas and other bugs. I get motion sickness riding horseback, really I do."

King Irv burst into laughter at this point. "Hershel, if you don't wish to make this journey just say so. It won't help your case much, but at least I'd like to know your honest feelings."

"Alright, Irv," Hershel shouted back. "I really don't want to make this journey," which earned him stern eyes from his monarch. "Uh, but I will, uh, if your highness thinks it's necessary."

"That's better, Hershel," King Irv soothed. "The trip shouldn't be so bad and you'll be home in your little cave before you know it, working on all your many projects."

"If you say so, highness."

King Arthur's face brightened into a big smile while Hershel's clouded over in despair.

Two mornings later, King Arthur's small group of knights had to stop by the Merlin's cave on their way out of town to awaken him, then they waited around for an hour or two, nervous horses prancing about along the second fairway of King Irv's golf course, while Hershel packed a small bag, complaining all the while that he didn't feel up to such a long and tiresome journey.

Arthur, on the other hand, was in great spirits. He was already anticipating that Hershel would whip his own magician back into shape, persuade his wife, by words or spells, to come back to his bed, and convince the local Christians as to the authenticity of the Holy Grail thingy. In his mind, Arthur was already adding up all his new-found blessings in the plus column of his ledger. Life would, once again, be as good as it used to be.

Among his luggage, Hershel counted two large firkins of ale which required a special horse to balance the two heavy barrels on either side of the saddle. At every stop along the way, the Merlin would fill his clay travel cup, seldom offering to share with anyone else in the caravan, which didn't make any friends among King Arthur's entourage. By the plains of Gloucestershire, Arthur's men were getting fed up with this man who drank constantly and complained incessantly about the hardships of the journey. When they reached the village of Exeter, Arthur almost had a mutiny on his hands but he coaxed his men onward, with no help from King Irv's man of magic. On the sixth day they crossed the Dart moor and dropped down into Cornwall. Hershel had run out of his own special ale and was requiring frequent stops at local public houses, none of which seemed to meet his expectations.

It was a miracle when they finally crossed the long bridge to Tintagel Castle without any casualties. Arthur showed Hershel to a special guest room in his seaside castle and, when the man of magic was settled in, guided him to Sten's secret cave that led down through the cliffs to Tintagel beach. Hershel proceeded cautiously down the steep, descending the tunnel with only a candle to light his way. He breathed a deep sigh of relief when he finally saw the dim light from the opening at the bottom of the palisades. He ventured forth onto the sand, blinking rapidly in the sunlight after his long passage through the dark cave.

Glancing west across the waves, Hershel could see Sten and four or five others sitting astride crudely carved surfboards in the small swells. One of the men shouted something and King Arthur's Merlin shaded his eyes with his left hand, scoping out the beach before him.

When his eyes came to rest on King Irv's Merlin, he shouted, "Hey, Hershel. Is that you?" The magician/surfer then burst into wild laughter and began paddling madly toward the shore. "Hershel, old buddy," he screamed, "I'm so glad to see you."

Upon reaching the beach, the Arthurian Merlin pulled his surfboard high enough up the sand to secure it from washing away and ran up the slope to throw his arms around his fellow man of magic.

"I'm so happy that you introduced me to this surfing wheeze," he shouted almost straight into Hershel's ear. "This is my true life's calling. Nothing in the world is as exciting to me as riding the wild surf."

"But, what about your service to your monarch?" Hershel inquired. Aren't you supposed to be providing science and magic so King Arthur's people can survive and prosper?"

"Feck that," Sten laughed. "It's time I lived a bit for myself."

FORTY-FOUR

"**S**o you've spoken with Sten?" Arthur asked Hershel when he found the man of magic drinking ale with whiskey shots in his parlor.

"I've spoken with him," Hershel replied, staring down into his litre- sized tankard.

"And you've talked him around," Arthur beamed with bright eyes.

"I've spoken with him," Hershel mumbled. "And I think I wasted my breath. Sten seems to have gone 'round the twist. He says he's no longer interested in science or magic. He just wants to hang out at the beach and ride waves. He's busy trying to encourage the fair ladies of your kingdom to dress in these skimpy clothes that are known in the future as 'bikinis' and he calls them all 'beach bunnies.' And I can't find any magic strong enough to turn his head around. Sorry, your highness."

King Arthur's face quickly drooped from grin to frown. He raised his hand to his staff for a pint and a shot of his own. "So, what are we to do?" he voiced in a sort of defeated lament. "Do you see no path of hope?"

"Path of hope?" Hershel replied. "There is always hope. Give me a day or two to think on this, I'll have some answers when next we meet. In the meantime, keep me well supplied with whiskey and ale, so my mind doesn't become dehydrated."

King Arthur scratched his head, but in the end relented. He'd already lost one Merlin, so he'd better humor the one remaining to him if he wanted some clear answers.

But was Hershel truly working to help him or was he only here to further some evil plan of that Jewish monarch, Irving? Life was so complicated.

Arthur walked back to his private quarters, which seemed so stark and empty with his lovely Guinevere gone. What did she see in Lancelot and all this Christian mumbo-jumbo anyway? Wasn't he, Arthur, the King, ruler over all his lands? The man who could give her everything material that she might desire? He tossed and turned through another sleepless night. In the morning, he decided to seek out Hershel once again. All this uncertainty had to stop!

Arthur found Hershel in the stables, seeming to be carrying on a conversation with one of his horses. The king was too far away to hear their words clearly, but he was sure Hershel and his livestock were talking about him. Was one of his horses the devil incarnate? The ultimate embarrassment, was there no shame in this world?"

Upon seeing him, Hershel turned with a wide grin and a bountiful greeting. "We were just talking about you, your highness," he chortled.

"Talking with whom?" Arthur asked, then glancing past Hershel, he saw the priest from the neighboring community and one of his novices.

"These good Christians are thinking that they'd like to take a second look at the Holy Grail cup you're offering," Hershel grinned.

"That would be nice," Arthur grinned. "Should I go and fetch it?"

King Irv and the Holy Grail

"Ah, highness," Hershel answered with a wink, "I think we should set up a formal viewing. I'll schedule this for you. There may be more than one interested party."

The king's face started with confusion but quickly brightened into a knowledgeable smile. "By all means, Hershel just let me know the time and place. I'd like to be in attendance at this event."

"My good king," the Merlin fired back, "You're scheduled to be the *host* to this event. We'll hold it on the cliffs across from your Tintagel Castle in a fortnight."

While Hershel spread the word about a showing of the Holy Grail, he was also busy in what had previously been Sten's workshop. He gathered what he could of rhinestones and costume jewelry to glue onto the rather plain grail cup. On a trip to a neighboring Christian kingdom to put up some handmade posters about the auction of the holy cup, he was able to procure a small golden cross that he pressed into the cup's side. When he was finished, it looked very much like the Holy Grail that Rutherford was circulating around the museums of the future world.

When the big day arrived, King Arthur found a dozen or more Christian rulers from as far away as Ireland and Wales camped on the meadow by the bridge to Tintagel Castle. Patrick of Ireland had pitched his broad marquee closest to the castle entrance.

"See here, Arthur," the man shouted as the king crossed from his home to survey the contestants. "What's the deal with you? This Holy Grail you are offering now looks nothing like what you offered me six weeks ago. How can I trust you to provide anything that might be real or true?"

At this point, Hershel came forward. He was dressed in a bright white robe with sky blue trim along the sleeves and hem, with a matching blue Star of David on the chest plate and a similarly blue yarmulke on the crown of his head. "This is Hershel, the Merlin of Irving, King of the Jews. King Irv is a direct descendant of a Jewish family from the time of your savior. His family rescued this special cup, from which the savior drank wine, on the night of the Last Supper. It has been in his family all these years.

"He has decided that he no longer wants the responsibility of being custodian of this holy relic. He would like it to have a home among people of the Christian faith as a gesture of his friendship. Along with your monetary offer, King Irv would also demand that the Christians that take possession of this Holy Grail pledge to always live in peace with those who have differing beliefs from their own, which is to say that you will no longer harass Druids, Jews, sun-worshipers or any others to try and convert us to your own peculiar beliefs. Now, who will bid on this item?"

Patrick stepped forward. "The good Christian people of Ireland will start the bidding with an offer of five pounds of the purest gold," he shouted.

At this statement, many of the other assembled monarchs shook their heads and backed away. Five pounds of gold? Who had a treasury that could afford such a price outside of the church itself?

Arthur stepped forward to address Patrick. "If I accept your offer of this gold, I will also demand the return of my wife, Queen Guinevere."

"I'll agree to that," Patrick told him. "The woman is a true pain in my side with her continual whining. You can have your good knight Lancelot as well."

Arthur gave out with a good and hearty laugh. "I've no use for a faithless knight, my friend. You may keep Lancelot and do with him as you please."

FORTY-FIVE

At that very moment, Anne of Rexia and her ladies were heading south from their West Yorkshire, uh, kingdom with a message of praise for King Irv and his wisdom. "Our ladies had a wonderful experience in dealing with this Holy Grail thing," she told Irv when he met her at the gates of his castle. "As soon as I explained what we had, and, of course parroted some Bible knowledge that my girls had picked up along the way, we had an easy time trading our grail to the local Christian kingdoms for a broad and sweeping peace agreement. All of a sudden, it was like we were a part of their crazy holy plan.

"The priest that presides over the cathedral in York is a firm believer in a humble Jesus, who would very much have drunk from a plain clay vessel."

"Please, don't tarry on my doorstep," King Irv beamed. "Bring your people inside. Let me fetch you all some ale."

"Wine for me, if that's okay," came a meek voice from the back of the group. As the man strode forward, Anne announced, "Good King Irv, may I introduce Friar Paul, the abbot of the Christian cathedral of York."

"This is an unexpected pleasure," King Irv beamed. "You must stop and visit the cathedral in our neighboring kingdom of Vaude while you're here."

"Thank you, kind sir," the man of God replied with a broad smile. "I bring blessings to your kingdom. I understand from my friend Anne that you are Jewish. I know our savior was a Jew, just as you are, my friend, and that it was the *Romans* who killed our lord. There is no rational reason why we, Christians and Jews, should not live in peace and support each other."

"Our Rabbi will be pleased to hear this," Irv replied. "In the meantime, my house is your house. Please make yourself at home here. We will prepare special guest quarters for you and your friend Queen Anne."

"I need no special quarters," Friar Paul replied. "I'm a humble man of God, and just as comfortable in your stables as anywhere else."

"We can't have that," spoke Prince Sol, stepping forward. "Let me show you to the Vaude Cathedral, where my friend Friar Agnello will see to your comfortable lodgings."

"You are most kind, good sir," Paul replied with a low bow. Turning to Anne, he asked, "Is it acceptable to you that I should leave your side and bunk in with the local priest?"

"I should want nothing less for you, my kind friend," Anne told the man of God.

On the following morning, Friar Paul and Queen Anne attended a breakfast on the Warehouse Castle bailey. Rabbi Weiss was there along with Giovanni Agnello, King Irv, Irv's son, Prince Sol, and King Richard of Vaude.

Irv's staff had prepared a special buffet, featuring a large assortment of dishes, including bagels with lox, poached eggs over bacon and biscuits and the usual English fry up of eggs, baked beans and tomatoes. Friar Paul dug in with gusto, as did Friar

King Irv and the Holy Grail

Agnello and the other Christians in attendance. King Irv and Queen Sophie nibbled at the lox and bagels while assessing their crowd of visitors. Queen Anne's ladies tucked in to the fresh vegetables on offer; broccoli, cauliflower and assorted squashes, shunning any meat products.

When the dishes were taken away, Friar Paul cleared his throat, then asked, "My good king Irv, how did you happen to come by the cup that refreshed our savior? So many of our good Christian brothers have searched to find this treasure, but to no avail."

"You'd have to ask Hershel, my Merlin," Irv beamed back at him. "Hershel is a remarkable man. He invented a time travel machine, in which he's gone both forward and backward through time.

"From the future, he's brought me ale in sealed tin containers as well as the game of golf and a very tasty dish we call pizza."

The Roman friar pressed back in his chair with a skeptical look. "Pizza? Tinned ale? A game? What does all this mean?"

"It's an amazing world out there," King Irv beamed. "More remarkable then we can ever know."

"Because of our Lord, Jesus," Paul put forth loudly.

"Well, maybe," King Irv grinned. "Or maybe just because that's the way the universe is structured. Rabbi Weiss nodded agreement. Friar Agnello sat behind them grinning. He was wise enough not to get involved in such a theological discussion.

"But surely," Friar Paul spit back at them, "all of this can only come from our Lord; Golf, pizza? It must all be a part of his magnificent plan!"

"Well, yes, it might be," Giovanni Agnello chuckled. "But what concern is this of ours? We'll just live the best lives we can and…"

At this point in the discussion, Prince Sol's wife, Princess Amy wandered into the room, her eyes dazed and her pace a slow, stumbling gait.

"What do any of you know of sin or of our Lord?" she shouted. "I talk to our Lord daily, and he hasn't any mercy to show any of you who cavort with *Jews*. Jews, like my father-in-law, destroyed our Lord to keep the people of our faith from attaining salvation! I've no love for any of you, including my so-called husband, the devil's front man. I will be married to our Lord, Jesus, the Christ, and none other. I call you all out as blasphemers."

There was a tense silence as Amy exited the room heading toward the old mill where once Wholesale's wise old historian, Mel of the Brooks, had lived. When Amy was out of sight, Prince Sol told them," I must apologize for my wife, the princess. I believe she has a screw or two loose in her head." The others nodded their head in agreement. "We will pray for her," Friar Paul offered with a troubled face.

The next morning, as Irv and Sophie came down to entertain their guests at breakfast, they found everyone had packed up and left in the night. Wendy, the serving wench, delivered a note from Queen Anne of Rexia. In a shaky hand Anne had written; My dear friend King Irv. I fear our relationship with Brother Paul has soured. He apparently had words with your Princess Amy yesterday and became very upset. We are returning to York at once so that I may negotiate with the Christians there before Brother Paul can poison their minds with the dark thoughts he says he received from your good Princess. Yours faithfully, Anne of Rexia.

FORTY-SIX

With an additional five pounds of pure gold in his treasury and Queen Guinevere back in his bed, King Arthur was once again a happy man. He pleaded with Hershel to stay on as his own Merlin, offering a considerable sum in gold, but the man who had invented time travel was anxious to get back to the Wholesale Kingdom and his own good king, Irv. King Arthur's many mood swings made him very nervous.

Angered at Hershel's departure, Arthur sent his knights down the bluffs to seize his own Merlin, Sten, for dereliction of duty and subversion against the good people of Cornwall. Sten was put under house arrest in his cave and his surfboard was burned along with all the other surfboards Arthur's knights could find along the Cornish coast.

Thinking about what King Irv had told him, Arthur sent a party east the next morning bearing bars of gold to look for a new inland seat for his government. A few miles east of the village of Glastonbury, one of the Christian areas that had been covered in his peace pact with Patrick, Arthur's knights were able to purchase some acreage atop a small hill just outside the village of South Cadbury.

Arthur followed his knights to this new area a few weeks later. The small rise, a sort of elevated mesa, would be easy to defend and offered an amazing view of the surrounding countryside. Arthur christened the hill "Camelot," the name King Irv had suggested, and he set his men to building a large new castle on the crest of the property. Arthur, Guinevere and the royal entourage set up large marquees around the outer edges of the mesa where they could camp as caravans were organized to bring all the royal property to the new locations. Life would be good here. Lancelot had been banished and, according to the Holy Grail pact, Patrick and all the other Christians would leave them in peace.

As construction was beginning on Camelot Castle, Hershel and his small group of accompanying Wholesale knights made their long journey back to the Irv's Kingdom from the west. The Merlin had very little good to say about Arthur or his western kingdom.

"The man locked Sten up in his cave, burned the man's surfboards and then had the nerve to offer me the job of being his Merlin… while he knew damn well that I'm loyal to you and Wholesale kingdom," Hershel later told his monarch. "As if I'd go to work for someone with such little respect for men of magic even if I didn't already have a gig!"

"Hershel, my friend," King Irv countered. "You're tired and angry from so many long days on horseback crossing our island from so far away. Let me fetch you a pint of ale and you can put your feet up and relax with me. Tomorrow we'll have a round of golf and everything will be good again."

"If you say so, highness," came Hershel's skeptical reply.

"Everything is satisfactory with the Holy Grail and this Christian fellow, Patrick, right?"

"It would seem so, Irv," Hershel chuckled as Wendy approached with a tankard of strong ale for him. "Though I don't know how far I'd trust those foreigners."

"Hershel," King Irv mocked, "Hasn't Rabbi Weiss taught us that all people are just that, people. We're all the same."

"Yeah, like the Canaanites," the Merlin muttered.

"Now Hershel," Irv chuckled. "That was way back in history, according to the Torah. We're much smarter and more civilized now."

"Let's hope so," Hershel told him, wiping suds from his lips after taking a long draught of ale, "for Arthur's sake.

Part Three
The Morning After

After a week or so of puttering around his laboratory, drinking the local ale and playing golf, Hershel was finally able to relax again and become his old, devil-may-care self. Bitter feelings about Arthur and his far off kingdom were forgotten. The Merlin spent some time hanging out with the Manischewitz brothers, helping them pick grapes, and he also passed some happy hours cleaning and polishing up his time machine.

Sipping Cabernet wine with the brothers reminded the Merlin that Rutherford and his Holy Grail world tour would be opening soon in Rome, in future time. "I think I need a little time travel holiday," Hershel told Irv while putting his ball into the cup of the ninth green. "I'm gonna set my course for modern Rome and see if I can catch up with the Metaphysical Brewing Tour while they're in Italy showing off the Holy Grail."

"Excellent idea," King Irv replied. "I'd like to know how things are going there myself. So far, from what I've heard, this has been very profitable for us. Is it September already? This year has just flown by."

"Anything special going on in the coming week?" he asked his king. "If not, I think I'll leave tomorrow right after breakfast."

Hershel's machine touched down on Via Crescenzio, just outside the Vatican walls. In the distance, he could hear loud shouting. He quickly disguised his time travel contraption as a large Fiat sedan and set off looking for the small church where he was to meet with Rutherford and the Holy Grail entourage. Approaching the structure, he heard a soft voice hissing his name.

"Rutherford, is that you?" he whispered loudly.

"In here," came the reply as the door to an old bakery across the square from the small chapel popped open just a crack. Hershel entered the bakery to find Rutherford standing behind the display cases with a large group of people crouched behind him. The Holy Grail was on the back counter behind them.

"What gives?" the Merlin asked in a casual voice.

"It's the Catholic Cardinals," one member of the group behind Rutherford told him. "They contacted us yesterday outside the Museum of Holy Souls in Purgatory. The Pope says that we must surrender the Holy Grail to his people. He has proclaimed that any such Christian relic belongs to the Mother Church. Fox News, a television station here in our times, got a hold of the story. They've stirred it up with the right wing Christians in America and now there's some kind of holy war brewing. Every Christian group is claiming ownership of the thing. We had a narrow escape from our hotel when the Vatican sent the mafia to steal the grail from us. They're searching for us door-to-door right now."

"Around here?" Hershel queried.

"Not yet," another voice told him. "We believe they're still searching around the city center, by the hotel where we were staying."

"So where's your machine parked?" Rutherford asked in a calm, assertive voice.

"About a block away, on a side street," the Merlin told him, "disguised as a large four-door Fiat."

Rutherford stepped forward with the Holy Grail in one hand and put his other arm around Hershel's thin shoulders. "Lead the way, Hersh," he barked. "The sooner we get this grail thing out of Italy and the future, the safer the entire world will be. My people are set to deny that such a thing ever existed. They'll all swear that our entire tour was a hoax."

"With all the publicity do you think anyone will believe that?" asked the incredulous Merlin.

"Maybe on our way out of here you can put some kind of spell on them?"

"Hey," Hershel countered, "Spells take time and planning."

"Just do your best, old friend," Rutherford breathed at him. "And hurry up getting back to the past. I think the Metaphysical Brewery Holy Grail Tour has come to an end."

FORTY-EIGHT

Rutherford breathed a sigh of relief as Hershel's machine deposited them in front of the Merlin's cave in *ancient* old blighty. "I'll tell you, Hersh, that was a really close one. I never thought that some old Christian relic would stir up that kind of fever."

"Whada ya mean?" Hershel asked.

"Well," Rutherford began hesitantly. "I just kinda thought everyone would be happy to see the thing, you know? To be able to brag to their friends and their children that they'd stood so close to something that they believed their religious leader or so-called savior had touched so many years before. Boy did I get a wrong number!"

"How so?" Hershel asked.

"First off," Rutherford told him, "while all these people *claim* to worship the same savior, every separate religious group wants to believe that they're the only ones in this so-called savior's eyes. All the other Christians, they say, don't count.

I didn't get this so much as the Holy Grail toured America, although there were some rumblings. The first hint was when the Church of England people in London started talking about the Lutherans as being 'late comers' to the faith, and that they, the Anglicans, should be entrusted as custodians of the relic. Then, in France, it started to hit the fan. When we left Chartres Cathedral, we started getting word of some strange messages coming out of Rome. The big fireworks started as soon as we landed at Leonardo da Vinci airport. There was a group of priests from the Vatican there as a welcoming committee. They offered to take us directly to the Holy See and put us up inside Vatican City, saying that they would take charge of the grail. When we told them we already had reservations in the city and two scheduled viewings for the Holy Grail before our Vatican engagement... Well, as soon as they left, we noticed we were being tailed by a group of unsavory characters in dark suits. Things went downhill from there."

Later, up at the castle, King Irv and his son-in-law had a private conference over a few pints of ale. Bird the cat sat, purring, in his master's lap. "So is this venture a total loss?" Irv asked.

"It's not all that bad," Rutherford chuckled. "By my last tally we'd cleared over half a million American dollars on the tour, and that's after we paid all the bills and gave more than half our take to various charities. I'm just worried that the tour ending so suddenly might hurt the Metaphysical Brewing Company's publicity. After all, they're the official sponsor."

"Hmm," the king mused. "I guess that's something to consider. Do you think people will really care that much or even remember?"

"We were hoping they'd remember the name of the beer," Rutherford stated before taking another drink from his flagon. "I've heard that remembering the name is the big thing. It may not matter if it's remembered in a positive or negative way, as long as the people remember it. My professors referred to that as something they called an attitude pie." He lifted his mug and took another drink. Bird seemed to nod positively, as though he understood exactly what was being said.

"Maybe the others in your group, the ones you left behind, will be able to put a positive spin on it," King Irv told him with a serious face.

"Let's just hope so," Rutherford groaned. "I should probably be getting back to check on everyone. They might be needing my help about now."

"Must you leave immediately?" Irv asked his son-in-law. "Sophie would love it if you could stay for dinner."

"Some other time, Irv," the dark scholar told him, "When I can maybe bring Judith with me for a day or two." He finished the last of his ale and held out his mug in salute to King Irv. "I'm off to find Hershel and my ride back to Rome."

Bird, the orange tabby, rolled over and looked to King Irv for a tummy rub.

FORTY-NINE

It was only three weeks after Rutherford returned the brewing company's Holy Grail from the future that some of King Arthur's men showed up at Warehouse Castle. "We bring sorrowful news from Camelot." Sir Galahad shouted up to the sentries on the walkway above King Irv's doorstep. "Please let us in. We must see King Irv at once."

"We have that Holy Grail thing with us," another knight shouted from the assembled troop. "King Arthur wishes to return it to you. It has caused him nothing but grief."

"Arthur believes the thing is cursed," added Galahad. "It holds some kind of evil Christian magic."

Irv sent one of the castle wait staff to fetch Hershel from his cave as he went forth to open the portcullis and deal with Arthur's knights. He also dispatched a rider to bring some of his own soldiers to the party. Hershel had recently told him not to trust this strange western king.

Irv needn't have bothered. When he had his men raise the heavy gate, he found Arthur's men quite meek, almost frightened. A young horseman that Irv didn't recognize came quickly forward and tossed the Holy Grail at Hershel's feet as through it were a smoldering ember.

"This Patrick fellow has our kingdom under siege," Galahad proclaimed loudly, shaking his head. "He came in the early dawn a fortnight ago with an army of Irishmen bearing banners sporting their big brown cross entwined with hawthorn branches Hawthornon a field of white. And he had other Christian leaders with him. They have all gone back on their words of living with us in peace. They're demanding our people leave this island."

"He said he drove the snakes from Ireland," came another voice from the pack, "and now he's come to drive the snakes from England as well, so he says."

"But how can this be?" questioned King Irv. "I thought this Holy Grail thing was supposed to be the key to all our peoples living together in harmony and understanding."

Galahad burst forth with a nasty laugh. "That's what these Christians tried to sell us," he barked. "And now they've kidnapped our good queen as well."

"So why are you not there helping defend good Arthur's kingdom?" Hershel asked.

"Our magnificent king was hoping that you and your fellows in Vaude could send reinforcements to our cause," another voice from the assembled knights shouted.

"Well," Irv dithered, "I must consult with my son, Prince Sol, and King John of our neighboring kingdom. We might be able to spare one or two regiments, but then who would we have to defend our own people from angry Christians?"

Sir Galahad lifted his helmet and scratched his head. "Are you under attack as well, sir?"

"We are currently safe," Irv told the men, "but if what you are saying is true, it's only a matter of time…"

Before Irv could finish his thought, he spied a large cloud of dust on the northern horizon. "My God," he exclaimed. "They might be coming for us as we speak."

Arthur's entourage turned their heads to follow King Irv's gaze, then quickly brought their horses around to that direction. The cloud grew larger and, within minutes, riders in armor could be seen coming down the King's Highway.

King Arthur's men dismounted and fell into a battle formation, their shields together in a wall that could forestall any breach of spears or arrows. King Irv's men quickly lowered the portcullis and raised the drawbridge before their main gate, then hurried up the stone stairs to the battlements.

But no arrows flew and no angry shouts were heard. From the heights of the castle walkways, Irv recognized a familiar face leading the charge toward his property.

"Don't shoot," he screamed through cupped hands, then one of his men brought a giant megaphone through which he repeated his command. "It's Queen Anne," he screamed at the top of his lungs. "It's Anne of Rexia, a friend."

FIFTY

"So I wasn't invited to the party," Anne quipped as she dismounted and signaled her ladies to stand by. "What's the occasion, anyway?"

"King Arthur is having some problems selling the idea of a Holy Grail," Hershel chuckled.

"Funny thing, that," Anne laughed back. "I'm here with a similar complaint. I thought this grail thing was supposed to buy us some respect... well, that ain't been happening."

"And I suppose you've brought your grail back to us as well?" Hershel smiled.

"We have," Anne told him in an angry voice, "and you can wipe that smile off your face. When we returned to York, our so-called friend brother Paul turned on us." Anne removed her helmet and looked deep into King Irv's blue eyes. "Your daughter-in-law, with her outburst, started our brother Paul thinking. Her tirade about Jews killing his so-called savior planted the seed in his pea brain. We weren't home ten days when the Bishop of York was on our doorstep demanding to know why we would accept a supposed Christian relic from a murdering Jew. Somehow, he'd become convinced that you Jews had stolen the thing while you were setting their Jesus person up to be crucified."

Irv shook his head, his lips and mustache drooping into a deep frown.

"So now, we have a major war brewing. These Christian have given us six months to get off *their* island or they will exterminate us to the last woman."

"Dear oh dear," Irv dithered. "Hershel, what can we do?"

Irv's Merlin stepped forward to address King Arthur's small band. "Galahad, sir, where is Sten?"

"Sten?" the lead knight inquired.

"Sten, King Arthur's Merlin. You know who I mean."

"I… I don't believe he's in good Arthur's employ anymore," Sir Galahad spit back. "He and our good king had a falling out."

"Well," Hershel fired back, "if you want to avoid an all out holy war, King Arthur better make peace with Sten first and then send him here to work with me. Together, we might be able to turn this situation around and save our unique, unchristian kingdoms. Without Sten's help, I can't promise anything."

"King Arthur is a proud man," Sir Galahad shouted back. "He will have to swallow some of that pride to bring Sten back into our fold."

"Then he'd better start swallowing," Hershel barked, "if he wants to save his kingdom and remain on our island."

There was loud, animated discussion among Arthur's knights, the horsemen moving around to speak with each other in the small assembly.

"May we stay here, in your protective kingdom for a few days?" Sir Galahad finally asked King Irv. "This is a lot to think about. We don't want to be thought as treasonous to our king, but we can understand that you have made a good point. We have much to consider here."

"You are welcome, as always, to camp in our northern fields, where you find the large stones," Irv told them. "Stay there as long as you like. But if we should be attacked, please let me count on you to stand with my own knights in defense of our Wholesale Kingdom."

Arthur's men gave this some thought. They hadn't come to defend another king's land, but at the same time, they didn't wish to die so many miles from their home. "We'll accept your terms," Sir Galahad finally told the Jewish monarch after conferring with his captains. "I believe our King Arthur would wish us to do just that, as we are not by his side to defend our own kingdom."

"Then you are welcome here as our guests and brothers," King Irv proclaimed. "And in return, I will do all I can to protect and defend my friend Arthur's little patch in the west. And I suggest that you send your fastest messenger out right away to ask your king to make peace with his old Merlin and then send him here to confer with my man Hershel. Time is of the essence."

![dragon] FIFTY-ONE ![dragon]

That evening, after Arthur's men and Anne's ladies had retired to the parade grounds north of his castle; King Irv held a quiet and secret meeting with King Richard of Vaude, his son, Prince Sol, his Merlin, Hershel and his inner circle of knights, including his Rabbi. Bird, the tabby, was listening in from his small bed in the corner of the room.

The topic of these Holy Grail things was foremost in their discussions, over and above the threat of holy war on the island or in future times.

"Maybe I didn't give the best counsel," Rabbi Weiss told the assembly. "My thoughts were somewhat clouded by Jewish thinking. I had no idea how crazy these Christians could be. I apologize to you, my liege," he bowed toward King Irv. "We teachers are, after all, only human. If we don't find a good answer in the Torah, well, sometimes we just have to wing it."

"Please, don't blame yourself, teacher," King Irv replied. "With Hershel's little machine taking us through time, well, we can't begin to know what to expect."

"That is a good *excuse*," the Rabbi told him, "but excuses are just that. They don't offer forgiveness, only an avenue to escape responsibility. We must find a way to make things right again, not excuse our wrongs." And with that, Rabbi Weiss turned on his heels and departed the meeting. The others continued to put their heads together to find a solution. Bird feigned sleep on his little cushion.

In the early morning, King Irv summoned Anne of Rexia and Sir Galahad to join him in a breakfast at Warehouse Castle. Hershel, his Merlin, was the only other person invited to the table. Irv waited in the wings until his guests were seated. He left them to ponder why they'd been summoned for some time, letting them speculate among themselves as to their presence at his table.

Irv entered the hall in full battle dress, sword at his side and helmet under his arm. Bird flew up from behind him to land masterfully on the long table before his monarch.

"You say that Christian kings are threatening your lands?" King Irv asked in a masterful voice. "And what are you prepared to do about this?"

Sir Galahad coughed and dithered while Queen Anne stood with a defiant look. "We came to you for support," the lady queen barked. "We look up to you as the strongest *un*christian monarch in our land."

King Irv gave a muted chuckle. "I'm no stronger than any of you," he told them. "I may be more *centered*, as I bear the faith of four thousand years of the struggle of my people. But then again, how many centuries have your people worshiped in your own faiths? Have you not faith in your sun goddess or the world of nature around you? Are not these beliefs as strong or stronger then some imported deity from a far-away land? Why do you not stand before your own gods, relying on the strength therein?" Bird rose up to stretch and gave them a stern look.

Irv's guests looked at each other, and then returned their eyes to the Jewish king. "You gave us these grail things," Sir Galahad whined. "To us, such a thing was little more than a rumor, or a fable, among our enemies."

"Some Christian ladies have run away from their husbands and rulers over the years to join our land," Anne piped up, "so I know a bit about Christian mythology, including this Jesus man's betrayal, last supper and crucifixion. I was always led to believe that they held this vessel in very high regard. Maybe it was just too much for them when non-believers possessed this thing they thought so sacred."

King Irv gave this some thought. "And while you're here," he asked, "who is defending your land?"

"Brother Paul is an educated and reasonable man," Anne told them, head held high. "He has granted us time to make arrangements to sail from England. The decree from his bishop states that if we are not gone before the first cold of winter, the church will rain down on us with the force of all the Christian men of York to kill us or drive us out. Their bishop says he doesn't really care which one it is."

"So you have some time to make plans," Irv said with a thoughtful pose. "And we have some time to deal with King Arthur's dilemma first."

"And I will lead my good women west in defense of Arthur if you, Galahad, will pledge to come to our defense once we've freed your Camelot of the threat of attack." Bird gave a positive cat-nod, then settled back for a short nap.

Sir Galahad leaned forward with his hand extended. "You have my word, good lady." When Anne extended her hand, Galahad leaned forward and kissed the back of her hand, like the knight and gentleman he was supposed to be.

King Irv loudly cleared his throat, then said, "With that settled, I will adjourn this meeting until two in the afternoon. When we reconvene out on the castle bailey, I will have my son and good King Richard present to offer what help they may in formulating our operation."

FIFTY-TWO

After ale was poured for all the assembled guests, King Richard stood to address the meeting. "Sometimes my father-in-law is too kind and trusting, too ready to lend aid to everyone around him. I don't see this as a fault, although it does cause some inconvenience to our conjoined kingdoms. My first thought here is that we must ask King Irving's Merlin, Hershel, to return these Christian Holy Grails to their rightful place in history. We can't erase the memory of these grail things from those in our time who have seen them, but we can hope that they dismiss what they've seen as some hoax or illusion. That will aid us in going forward."

All the gathered heads nodded at this, wearing grim faces.

"I've been told by King Irv that some of you are under a threat of annihilation if you do not abandon your lands and flee from our island. I do not command a powerful nation, but I will always stand for what is right! The Land of Vaude is committed to defending your rights. And I'm sure my father-in-law, King Irv, is just as committed to your cause.

"I also know that King Irv's Merlin, Hershel, is completely committed, and Hershel, being a man of magic, can give us aid on what we might call a supernatural level."

This brought smiles from the assembled knights and rulers.

"I will now turn this podium over to my father-in-law, King Irv, as he is the man that I know can make it all happen."

Irv took the stage with a somewhat puzzled expression, but Richard took his hand and squeezed it with a confident smile. Rabbi Weise, sitting in the wings, also gave Irv a wave and a smile of reassurance. Bird, feigning sleep in the Rabbi's lap, seemed to have no interest.

The good king's face was all a-beam by the time he faced his audience. He took a couple deep breaths and cast confident eyes at his assembled guests.

"So I have been labeled as too kind and too ready to help. I readily accept this mantle. Isn't that what a ruler of men should be? I always strive to be a mensch; someone my God will look down on and give a happy smile, especially in trying times like these. I only pray that I can live up to the confidence you have all vested in me."

This statement drew some confused looks, but the folks listening to him ended up smiling and giving positive nods. From his place in the Rabbi's lap, Bird gave a quick wink of his large yellow-green eye.

"My Merlin, Hershel, is still awaiting word from good King Arthur's man, Sten. When our two men of magic have had time to confer, we should have a strong defense that goes beyond the strength of numbered troops. That, plus the fact that goodness is on our side; all men deserve the right of self determination, the right to worship God in whatever fashion suits them and their lifestyle."

When the other leaders had left, Irv sat down with Hershel to assess their situation. Bird climbed into the king's lap and started purring. "What more can I do in this matter?" the monarch asked his Merlin. "What more can we do to prevent an all-out holy war?"

King Irv and the Holy Grail

"I don't know about a holy war here in our time, majesty, but to restore a balance in the universe, I think we need to unload these so-called Holy Grail things, and sooner, rather than later." Bird the cat raised his ginger head and nodded agreement.

"You believe them to be part of the problem?" King Irv asked his man of magic.

"They could be," Hershel replied, "but even if they aren't, why take a chance? I suggest that we remove all the extra jewels and adornments we put in these things and I take them back in time where they belong. It would be nice if I could erase everyone's current memory of the thing, but when the grails are gone, they'll probably forget about all this eventually. If they should ask us about it, we'll simply deny any knowledge. What-da-yah think?"

"Oh, I do wish Rutherford was here to consult with us."

"Believe me, highness, Rutherford would agree that we should dump these crazy vessels. You don't know the grief this Holy Grail thing caused him in future Roma."

King Irv thought for a minute, then asked, "How soon do you think we can get rid of them?"

"My time machine is less than a minute away, highness," Hershel replied with a wink. "I can pull the baubles and bangles off the cups in less than an hour. I'd say I can have them back in ancient Jerusalem before the sun comes up over the desert there."

"Then go now," Irv told him. "Go with all due speed and rid us of these cursed clay cups."

FIFTY-THREE

Hershel returned to his cave with the three grail vessels that had been given to him by the Christian savior. He popped the jewels out that had been superficially stuck on the surface of the three grails. The gold crosses, he quickly melted down into a tiny ingot for future use. When the clay vessels had been returned to their original state, he tossed them into a burlap sack and loaded that sack into his time machine.

Hershel set his machine's coordinates for Mordechai's All Kosher Grill and Bar, near the Temple on the Mount, in the year thirty one by the Christian calendar. "This is where these grail things rightfully belong," he told himself.

As luck would have it, he returned to the exact moment in time where he had received the grails in the first place. The Jesus person had just placed the three Holy Grails on the bus boy's dirty dish tray for Hershel to pluck and was turning to beat a hasty retreat.

On seeing Hershel over his shoulder, Jesus gave a quizzical look, turned and asked, "You're still here?"

"Well," Hershel hesitated. "I kinda left but then I came back... Ugh, to check on you? You doin' okay?"

"Hey, I'm fine," the savior answered. "Like, we were just talking a minute ago. So why did you really come back, Hersh?"

"Well," he dithered, "ah, it's like this, uh."

"Come on, out with it man! No need to play games with me. I gave you those cups that you were supposed to take to the future to secure my legacy."

"Well," Hershel answered in a shaky voice, "it, uh, didn't work. The cups just caused more fighting and confusion, so I brought them back. They're over there with the dirty dishes, if you really must know. One of them has a shiny glaze on it, but otherwise, they're just like you gave them to me."

"A shiny glaze?" Jesus asked, tilting his head with an inquisitive look.

"Don't ask," Hershel replied. "You don't want to know."

At this, Jesus burst out in laughter. "Best laid plans of mice and men," he roared.

"Uh, I'll have to remember that one," Hershel confessed. "It's pretty good. But I don't think I can give you credit if I use it. No one would understand."

"Fine by me," the savior told him. "I'm hoping to be remembered by much more important words than those. Now get out of here before these crazy Romans see me talking to you and use it to trump up more charges against me."

Hershel gave the man a military salute then turned on his heel and got back in his tin egg for the journey back to old England.

The Merlin was back in old blighty almost before he had left, facing an anxious King Irv that paced before his cave with an orange tabby cat on his heels.

"Everything went okay?" the monarch asked.

"Just like we planned," Hershel told him. "And you know, that Jesus cat is really pretty cool. Too bad his followers have made him into something scary."

"Not our concern," Irv replied. "We'll just listen to our Rabbi and live the best life we can."

"If you say so," the Merlin replied.

"Hershel," the king stated with a pained expression, "you aren't thinking of joining these Christians, are you?"

The Merlin hesitated a minute, then answered, "Ah, you know me, Irv. I'm a man of science. I have a hard time with things accepted on faith. You've got to show me the facts. And if I can't follow a logical path to a conclusion, I ain't buying."

After King Irv returned to Warehouse Castle, Hershel returned to his cave, poured himself a generous tankard of ale, and surveyed the projects lined up on his desk. There was no big hurry on his commission to put a spell on certain chickens or ducks that they might lay eggs of pure gold. He had to laugh at the local farmers that wanted to believe such a thing could be done. He also laughed at his commission from certain wealthy folks that desired a spell to turn water to wine. "Yeah," he murmured aloud, "Like they're too cheap to give our local vintners their due."

At the far end of his work table, Hershel noticed an old idea he'd toyed with from time to time; an invisibility spell. Could he incant certain words to make himself, or others close to him, cloaked so as not to be seen by the eyes of their enemies? That might be a big help to King Irv and the other non-Christian kings should this grail wheeze come to some sort of holy war.

"Sten and his King Arthur would like this one," he chuckled to himself. "Irv would be impressed as well." Yes, this was where he should focus his studies.

FIFTY-FOUR

Hershel focused on this new invisibility spell with all his heart and soul. He had no idea how long he'd been bent over his desk formulating algorithms that could apply to human forms, but when he finally emerged, he found King Irv's army in full battle dress heading for the highway west toward Cornwall.

"Hershel," his monarch cried, "Patrick and the Christians have attacked King Arthur's Camelot. We've no time to lose. Are you joining us?"

"Have we heard anything from Sten?" the Merlin shouted back.

"I've had no word as to Sten's presence, but there's a good chance he'll be there when we arrive to help Arthur. So are you with us?"

"I'll just be a minute, highness. I've got something that might help turn the tide." Hershel mentally went over what he had of his spell to make men invisible. "I'll mount up and follow behind your troops as soon as I've gathered some important papers."

As his eyes rose to meet those of his king, he couldn't help but notice a large ginger tabby head poking up from the monarch's saddlebags. The king's cat, Bird, had elected to join the fight.

Back in his laboratory, Hershel went over his figures one more time. His spell of invisibility could work, in theory, on a small group of people. If he could just choose the right group of soldiers, his newest invention could possibly turn the tide of a battle. As backup, he could always move men around with his time machine. Yes! His time machine.

Hershel mounted up on a swift mare and raced forward to speak to King Irv.

"Highness," he shouted. "Highness, hold up for a moment and listen to me."

The army was moving slowly toward the main east-west highway, so Hershel was able to catch up quickly. "Highness," he shouted again and again until he saw King Irv's head swivel around toward him. "Highness, I've got a plan. How long will it take your good knights to reach Camelot?"

Irv halted the procession, turned his mount to face his Merlin and gave a thoughtful pose. Bird poked his ginger head from the saddlebag to see why they had suddenly halted.

"You have good news for me, Hershel?" the king called out.

"Maybe," his Merlin answered. "I'm not sure. But instead of riding out with your troops, if you'll tell me approximately when you'll arrive in Camelot, I'll tweak my time thingy so I'll be there when you arrive. With my time egg at the battle sight, I might be able to perform some tricks of subterfuge that will help our cause."

"That's an interesting idea," King Irv replied, sticking a finger under his helmet to scratch his brow. "Is there something specific that we should be looking for when we arrive at King Arthur's place?"

"I'm not sure yet," Hershel replied. "I'll know more when I can hook up with Sten. According to some calculations I just made, I might be able to turn some of your good knights invisible so they can pass through the Christian lines to fight unseen. If that doesn't work, I might be able to use my time machine as a weapon to support our side."

King Irv gave a broad smile. "Hershel, you never cease to amaze me. God speed and good luck to you. I'll see you in Camelot in a fortnight," the king said with a crisp military salute.

FIFTY-FIVE

Kings Irv and Richard rode hard toward the west, almost a week in the saddle with minimum rest between sunset and sunrise each night. Their small army gave no complaints. They were fired up and ready to fight these Christian usurpers, even though many of King Richard's knights were, themselves, Christians. The very thought that someone might try to deny self-determination to any of the good people of their island simply rubbed the wrong way. Christian, Jew, Wicken or Druid, every man that lived under the rule of law on this isle called England deserved to be treated with respect and dignity. They would accept nothing less! And so the fever grew each night around the campfires as the men shared stories about their own beliefs, their lives and their families.

The assembled knights of Wholesale and Vaude arrived outside Camelot with froth on their lips and steel in their sword-bearing arms. Hershel and Sten were there to greet them, cleverly disguised as pig farmers, complete with the pong of mud-soddened pork on their tunics.

"Excuse the smell, highness," Hershel chuckled. "With these stinky outfits, we've managed to do some reconnoitering among the Christian invaders. We've sorted out their strengths, which are mainly their faith in this Jesus character and his incarnate representative, Patrick, and their weaknesses, which are almost too many to list.

"This Christian army has been cobbled together from a lot of different tribes and villages, many whom have been enemies throughout recorded time. They don't even communicate in a common tongue. Some speak Gaelic, others an off-shoot of Welsh, and many talk in various dialects of English. They're united as Christians, but extremely mistrustful of one another."

"But they are fighting for a common cause," King Irv stated bluntly.

"Well, yeah," his Merlin answered, "until something might come up to highlight their mistrust of each other."

"Something like what?" Irv asked loudly.

"Something like, maybe, a red devil jumping out of a tin egg," Hershel grinned. "A devil praising Patrick as his employer... A devil cheering them on as his own representatives..."

King Irv shook his head. "Hershel, old son, pardon my saying so, but you are one devious bastard!"

"Thank you, my liege," Hershel replied with a grin and a slight bow. "We haven't been able to test it yet, but I think Sten and I might be able to make the front line of your troops invisible as well. If this wheeze works in real life as it seems to in theory, Patrick's front line will be totally confused by a line of swords and shields coming at them with no physical bodies attached. Of course, your men will be there, but Patrick's men won't be able to see them."

"Most remarkable," Irv said, incredulity written across his face. Bird, the tomcat slowly arose from the king's saddlebag and raised a ginger paw in a military salute.

King Irv and the Holy Grail

As per the instructions of King Arthur's Merlin, Sten, and Kings Richard and Irv set up their encampment in a thick forest just south of the hill on which Camelot had been constructed. Hershel's intelligence had selected the spot as most of Patrick's troops were waiting within easy striking distance to the northern forecourt of Arthur's castle. Both Sten and Hershel continued to tramp about in their pig-man outfits keeping tabs on the enemy. Before dawn, they had prepared a report for their kings on the approximate number of knights in Patrick's army, their strength in weapons and the number of horses their army could mount.

At first light, Patrick's rag-tag Christian army began their march up the hill to Arthur's Camelot, loudly chanting slogans and singing songs about their savior. King Irv watched from the high battlements of King Arthur's castle. His first observation was that Patrick's troops seemed quite lacking in military knowledge or bearing. As they moved forward, with Arthur's former faithful knight, Lancelot front and center, no one guarded their flanks or watched their rear. It seemed more like a group of school bullies trying to intimidate a lone, weak child. King Irv turned a broad smile toward his host.

"You find this amusing?" Arthur asked his fellow monarch.

"Actually, I do," Irv replied. "These men are just some sort of fired-up rabble, kind of like an angry mob. There is nothing noble or military about their formation. They may believe they have some kind of God on their side, but in truth, they're more like lemmings marching into a wild, frothing sea. If your men can't defeat this band of half-wits, then you've no right to rule over them."

King Arthur wheeled on Irv with a red face and an angry expression. "How dare you question my abilities?"

At this, Irv laughed. "I'm not making any judgment as to your expertise," he told his friend, "merely making an observation. This is no *army* attacking you, it's merely a group of farmers fired up by some loudmouth blowhard. I'm afraid all your worries have been in vain, my friend. I'm only sorry that your trusted fellow Lancelot would do you such an injustice as to lead your enemies against you."

"But they're attacking my castle," Arthur fired back. "They're threatening Camelot."

"Yes, they would appear to be," King Irv said with a nod of his head. "But in truth, I don't see any real threat here." And with that, Irv nodded to the aide by his side who fired a flaming arrow into the air, the sign for Hershel, Sten and the other kings to set their plan into action.

From the thick forest to the south of Camelot, the combined forces of Vaude and Wholesale began their march forward. The troops split into two groups, knights of Vaude to the left of the rise on which Arthur's castle stood, King Irv's men to the right. At the same time, Hershel's tin egg appeared in the center of Patrick's front line, the Merlin emerging dressed all in red, sporting fake horns and a long crimson tail.

Almost immediately a large number of Patrick's men fell to their knees uttering loud prayers for salvation. The others slowed their forward progress, looking all around themselves for some kind of sign.

King Irv and the Holy Grail

The few who continued to march forward toward Camelot, led by Sir Lancelot and unaffected by this scene, soon encountered two lines of swords and shields coming toward them from both sides of the field with no physical bodies attached.

While Patrick, guiding the battle from behind his troops, shouted for them to soldier on, he watched his brave Christian soldiers flying north past him in a hasty retreat. Lancelot shouted, "Cowards! Come back and fight like men. Does our savior mean so little to you?"

King Arthur, with the help of Kings Irv and Richard, had defeated the Christian forces with very little loss of life or injury. Those who died were mostly Christians trampled by their own retreating forces. The three kings stood on the battlements of Camelot watching the retreat of Patrick's army. Bird the cat walked along the parapet wall with a smug expression and a wildly waving orange tail. He meowed a loud cry of victory.

King Arthur sent for three mugs of ale to celebrate just as Hershel and Sten appeared at the head of the staircase. Arthur rushed forward to throw his arms around his Merlin. "Better make that five ales," he shouted.

"Sten, my old friend," he cried as he hugged his long-time man of magic, "I'm so sorry that I ever doubted you. Would you please return to my service at once? I'll give you anything you need to carry out your experiments."

Sten fought the smile that wanted to play on his lips, "Anything, highness? Like maybe I can keep a lab at Tintagel and do a bit of surfing from time to time?"

"Surfing? Of course! Whatever it takes to keep your amazing mind cranking at full speed."

Hershel shot Sten a wink from across the battlements. Hopefully, they could do some work together in the future. Sten wasn't such a bad guy, when it came right down to it.

FIFTY-SIX

Knights from all three kingdoms followed the trail of Patrick and his men back to the Cornish coast, where they were seen to board boat after boat. Their exodus lasted much of the day. When the last Irish Christian and a large number of the English island followers of the Irish priest had sailed west, the combined English forces rode back to Camelot to report that all was now safe. It could be assumed that the Christians of Ireland would not be back anytime soon.

The next day, King Arthur threw a gala the likes of which had not been previously seen anywhere in the west of their island. Royal servants and local merchants alike erected wide marquees across the plateau of Camelot selling roasted game hens, braised cow ribs, all manner of sweet cakes and pies, and lots of strong ale. The veterans of the short Christian war were all awarded medals of valor and bravery by Arthur as well as by their own monarchs in a ceremony at mid day. After that, all those wearing the new medals were given all the free ale they could drink.

Late in the afternoon, from the midst of the drunken revelry, a lady appeared riding side-saddle on a silky white mare, prancing towards the small raised dais where the three kings watched over the events. As she came closer Arthur stood and exclaimed, "My God, I believe that is my unfaithful wife, Guinevere. What is she doing here?"

Skoot Larson

The lady rode side-saddle right up to the low stage and dragged herself from her mount to the boards before her king. She crawled to his feet, keeping her eyes averted from his.

"My dear husband who I have so wronged," she wailed in a voice choked by tears. "Woudst thou ever consider taking me back into your good graces? I'm so sorry for my unfaithfulness. I now realize what a good and kind man you are. And I see these Christians for the charlatans they have been, along with that self-serving coward Lancelot."

King Arthur fought to hold a stern face and hide the grin that wanted to creep across his face. "You would agree to renew our vows of marriage before all our kingdom and assembled guests?" he asked.

"Oh yes," she cried, raising her eyes to meet those of her husband.

Arthur could no longer hold back his smile. He leaned forward, grabbed Guinevere's hands and pulled her up to his embrace.

"Your word is enough, my queen," he breathed, holding back tears of his own.

"Giles, Reginald, bring a chair for my wife and queen." Arthur shouted. Then he stood and showered his Guinevere with kisses while his men brought forth a suitable throne for his newly reunited lady.

🐉 EPILOGUE 🐉

When Hershel's time machine returned to the Wholesale Kingdom, he headed straight into the village for a pint of strong ale to get his head together. Upon entering the Wholesale Public House, Morrie the Jester hailed him from the back of the room. Hershel had second thoughts about speaking with the neighboring kingdom's jester and funny man, but he dutifully carried his drink to where he was summoned.

"So why do noblemen wear red garters?" Morrie the Jester asked Hershel the Merlin.

"Uh, to keep their socks up?" Hershel answered without hesitation.

"Oh, I must have told you that one before," came Morrie's reply.

The two men were, once again, ensconced in the back booth of the Wholesale Arms, the public house in the little village near King Irv's castle and golf course where Hershel had first shared the news of the upcoming Merlin's convention with the comedian almost a year earlier.

"So are you ready for another pint?" Morrie asked, after draining the dregs of his own flagon. Hershel had hardly touched his own drink in spite of his need to relax after his ordeals in the Middle East and in Cornwall with King Arthur's troops. Morrie the Jester wasn't helping him any.

"No, I'm good," Hershel told the man. "I've still got things to do back at my cave before I stop by the castle to see King Irv. I gotta keep a clear head," he lied. "So what's new with you?"

"Well," Morrie trumpeted with a swelling chest, "I'm putting together a whole new act. It'll be the hit of the Midland's Circuit. Lots of killer diller new material."

"Oh yeah?" the Merlin replied with little interest as he took another sip of his own ale. "And where did you get this new material?"

"I haven't even looked through it all yet, but it is going to be hot, and *funny*! Really funny! There was this traveling salesman came through the kingdom last week, while you were off somewhere in that time thingy of yours."

"Really?" Hershel looked up in surprise, "A joke salesman?"

"Well, he had lots of different stuff on offer," Morrie told the Merlin. "But what got my attention? He had some ancient Greek scrolls, very old. He told me they used to belong to the greatest entertainer in the ancient world, Archomedian. You've heard of him, right?"

"Archomedian?" Hershel questioned, trying to keep a straight face.

"Yeah," Morrie beamed. "I can't wait to start putting some of this into my act."

"And you can read ancient Greek?" Hershel queried. "This stuff *is* all in Greek, isn't it?"

King Irv and the Holy Grail

"That's the beauty of it," Morrie beamed. "This Archomedian fellow had translated all his material into English. The guy said that the great man thought it lost something in the original."

"Sounds pretty amazing," the Merlin replied, holding back a threatening guffaw. "But, hey, listen, I gotta go now."

"But you haven't even finished your ale," Morrie barked.

"You finish it for me," Hershel sputtered, pushing his half full flask across the narrow table and stumbling toward the door.

Out in the street, Hershel could no longer control himself. He laughed so hard that he almost fell down and lost total control of his bladder, thankful he hadn't had any more ale.

"Oh what an idiot," he barked between fits of giggles. "I think maybe we should have sold Morrie the Holy Grail."

ABOUT THE AUTHOR

S koot Larson is a native Los Angelino, a musician, music critic and a Viet Nam veteran. He has also worked as a disc jockey, actor, speech therapist, stand-up comedian, behavioral counselor and streetcar conductor. His previous works include the Lars Lindstrom Zen-Jazz Mystery series, a black-humor novel about health care in America entitled "Apollo Issue," and a political humor novel, "The Palestine Solution." Skoot lives with his two cats in Rockport, Texas.